HIS FOURTH OF JULY BLESSING

LEE TOBIN McCLAIN

ISBN-13: 978-1-335-94042-1

His Fourth of July Blessing

Love Inspired
22 Adelaide St. West, 41st Floor
Toronto, Ontario M5H 4E3, Canada
www.LoveInspired.com

HarperCollins Publishers
Macken House, 39/40 Mayor Street Upper
Dublin 1, D01 C9W8, Ireland
www.HarperCollins.com

Printed in U.S.A.

1 2 3 4 5 6 7 8 9 10 HDC 28 27 26 25

"How'd you get so smart about parenting?" he asked finally.

"I was fortunate, having both parents." She frowned, looking at the ground. "Although…"

He could tell she had something more to say. "What?"

"My mom was just…" She trailed off and waved a hand. "I'll tell you the story sometime. I think my childhood was pretty good on balance, even though there were a few rough spots."

They walked on along the grassy path beside the river. A cool breeze lifted a lock of Kitty's hair, and Emilio wanted more than anything to reach over and tuck it behind her ear.

Which would be inappropriate. Wouldn't it? Was she feeling any of the same romantic vibes he was? Would she freak out if he touched her?

He forced his thoughts back to their conversation. "I guess nobody has a perfect childhood," he said. "But I want to make my nieces' childhoods as good as possible. I'll consider what you've said about Nora."

She smiled up at him. "You're a good man." She took his hand and squeezed it, and this time, she didn't let go.

Lee Tobin McClain is the *New York Times* bestselling author of emotional small-town romances featuring flawed characters who find healing through friendship, faith and family. Lee grew up in Ohio and now lives in Western Pennsylvania, where she enjoys hiking with her goofy goldendoodle, visiting writer friends and admiring her daughter's mastery of the latest TikTok dances. Learn more about her books at leetobinmcclain.com.

Books by Lee Tobin McClain

Love Inspired

Holiday Haven

A Home for Mother's Day
His Fourth of July Blessing

Tumbleweed, Texas

The Coach's Secret Child

K-9 Companions

Her Easter Prayer
The Veteran's Holiday Home
A Friend to Trust
A Companion for Christmas
A Companion for His Son
His Christmas Salvation
The Veteran's Valentine Helper
Holding Onto Secrets
Her Surprise Neighbor
An Unexpected Christmas Helper

Visit the Author Profile page
at LoveInspired.com for more titles.

Remember ye not the former things,
neither consider the things of old. Behold,
I will do a new thing; now it shall spring forth;
shall ye not know it? I will even make a way
in the wilderness, and rivers in the desert.
—*Isaiah* 43: 18–19

Dedicated to all veterans

Chapter One

Kitty MacIntyre felt her shoulders relax as she watched the last carful of tired, happy guests drive away. "I think our first weekend went well," she said to her father, who was sweeping the entryway of the Holiday Haven Guesthouse.

The sun shone low and golden on this Sunday evening, the last day of May. They'd managed to reopen the family guesthouse on schedule, and their first guests had loved it here. Kitty stretched her arms above her head, twisting her back from side to side, and then sank down on the bench just inside the front door.

"It did go well," her father said. "Wish you could take a break, but it looks like your next project is here."

Kitty's heart skittered. She stood and looked out the window at the SUV that was pulling into the space just vacated by their weekend guests.

This had to work, for her son's sake.

Not wanting her father to worry, she forced a confident, happy tone into her voice. "Emilio is just the person I need to put River Haven's Fourth of July celebration over the top."

"Maybe," Dad said doubtfully, looking out the window. "It looks like he has a lot on his plate. And you do, too, with keeping Mason busy and helping with the guesthouse. You sure you haven't bitten off more than you can chew, managing the Fourth of July event, too?"

"It'll be fine." She just had to get Emilio and his nieces moved in, get reacquainted with her old friend, and see if he could help her achieve her goal.

The front doorbell rang.

"You greet them," her father said. "I'll put cookies in the oven and then double-check their rooms. Looks like the older girl might be…" He frowned, shrugged and disappeared without finishing his sentence.

Kitty hadn't seen Emilio Mancini for almost five years, but they talked on the phone fairly often, especially since she'd gotten divorced and he'd become guardian to his nieces. He was her oldest and dearest friend, and she couldn't wait to see him.

True, inviting Emilio and his nieces to stay at her family's Western Pennsylvania guesthouse for the summer had been a fairly impulsive offer. But it was Emilio. Good old Emilio. It would work out.

She opened the door.

Her eyes traveled upward, and she sucked in her breath. Emilio looked…different. Taller. A squarer jaw. A more powerful build.

Wow.

She blinked and studied the two girls

standing beside him. The little one was an adorable, curly-haired toddler. The other was a preteen, wearing a short black dress, ripped fishnet stockings and heavy work boots.

"Hi! Welcome!" She held open the door and gestured for them to come inside.

They crowded into the foyer. Emilio had bags under his eyes and a weary expression. But he smiled at her with genuine happiness and reached out to give her a big hug. Emilio was Italian, and hugging was part of his makeup.

Feeling his strong arms wrap around her made Kitty suck in a quick, deep breath. Again, she had the impression that he'd changed. But of course, his years of active military service had made him broader-shouldered and more muscular than when she'd last seen him.

She stepped back and knelt to greet the little girl. "Hi! Welcome to Holiday Haven. I'm glad you're here."

The toddler stared at her with wide eyes,

then stuck her thumb in her mouth. She didn't speak.

Emilio put an arm around the taller girl's shoulders, which the girl promptly shrugged away. "This is Nora," he said, giving her another quick side squeeze. "She just finished sixth grade." He put a hand on the little girl's head. "And this is Alice. Girls, meet my best friend from way, way back. Kitty Wright."

"Kitty MacIntyre," she murmured. "I kept my married name so it would be the same as Mason's."

His eyebrows lifted, just a fraction. "Right. Sorry to forget."

The black-clad teen glared at her uncle and spoke for the first time. "Your best friend is a woman? You didn't say that before. Come on, Alice. Let's get out of here."

Alice immediately lifted her arms, and Nora picked her up, staggering a little with the weight of the chubby toddler. They were out the door and headed toward the road before either Kitty or Emilio could react. A passing car swerved around them with a friendly honk.

"Get back here, Nora!" Emilio shouted. "Sorry," he said to Kitty and strode after the two girls.

"Wait." Kitty followed at a jog and tapped his shoulder. "Don't yell at her."

He stopped and turned back, his eyes dark and puzzled.

"She's scared for some reason." She passed Emilio and hurried toward the girl, whose pace was slowing.

A train chugged by on the track across the street. On their side of the road, at the edge of the trees, a deer lifted its head and looked at them calmly.

The twelve-year-old stopped. "Look, Alice," she said in an awestruck whisper.

Alice squealed, and the deer bounded away.

Kitty took advantage of the girls' pause to stand in their path, blocking them from going farther. "Hey, it's good to meet you. You're going to have a fun summer here."

The older girl sneered. But there was

something else beneath it. Those eyes, dark like Emilio's, held insecurity and fear.

Kitty wanted to connect with Nora, but as a middle school teacher, she knew twelve-year-olds weren't easy. The key was to keep talking, let them know you were friendly rather than judgmental. "Your uncle and I used to play all around here with our friends." Kitty waved an arm to encompass the lawn, the river and the railroad tracks. "The two of us were best buddies."

Nora let her sister slide to the ground and looked at Kitty, frowning. "A boy and a girl, best buddies?"

"Because of our moms," Kitty explained. "They were close friends." She wondered why that was a sticking point for the girl.

And then it dawned on her. This child was scared by the idea that she and Emilio might be more than friends. Emilio had told Kitty that the girls' mother had left the state with a boyfriend, the last in a long line of them.

Maybe Nora had internalized the idea that adults in love relationships would leave them. No wonder she didn't like the idea of Emilio, the only relative who'd been willing to take them in, being somebody's boyfriend. "We're just friends," she said firmly.

Emilio had come up behind his nieces but stayed a few steps away, listening.

Kitty kept her gaze on the older girl. "We never even went on one date."

"Really?" The girl's heavily made-up eyebrows lifted.

"Really. I love him dearly, but he's not my type." Kitty didn't have a type, not anymore. And after her disastrous marriage, she wasn't going to seek one out. "Why don't you come on back inside and see where you'll be staying? Maybe you could even have some chocolate chip cookies, if that's okay with your uncle."

Emilio laughed, a rich, deep, throaty sound. "If they're your mom's recipe, I call the first five cookies."

That made Kitty smile. "Both our moms

used to scold him for eating so many cookies," she said to the girls.

"Cookies!" Alice said. It was the first Kitty had heard her clear, high voice. The little girl looked up at her sister. "Can we?"

Kitty's heart lurched. The toddler hadn't consulted Emilio, hadn't even looked at him. She'd asked her sister.

Kitty had seen this behavior before: siblings parenting each other. Kids who took on responsibility way too young, usually because their actual parents were unwilling or unable to do their job.

Emilio *did* have a lot on his plate, if that was the situation. "I'll go get out cookies and milk," she said and headed back toward the guesthouse, leaving Emilio to handle the girls.

She wanted to help, but she didn't want to take over. Emilio had to figure out how to care for his new little family. That was the reason he'd called her, and the reason she'd extended her invitation. He lacked confidence in his parenting ability, and she'd promised to coach him. Being the mother to one child and the teacher of many, she had the experience Emilio lacked.

As she lifted warm cookies off the baking trays and onto a serving plate, she thought about the past she shared with Emilio. His mom had been fun and funny, and Kitty's own mother had adored her. They had been the two unconventional moms, cutting up at parent meetings, making silly jokes and dressing more like old-fashioned hippies than traditional, conservative parents.

Now, they were both gone. Kitty swallowed hard.

Emilio's sister, older than him, had been nice, too, and a lot of fun. But both she and her mother had lacked something, some kind of certainty or confidence. Maybe a moral compass. They'd been vulnerable to any man who paid them attention, and they had both gotten into trouble as a result.

Kitty remembered her own mother counseling Emilio's mother and sympathizing with her when one of her relationships had gone south.

Not that Kitty's mom had been flawless in the moral department.

Kitty pushed that thought away. She was still getting used to what she'd learned about her mother just a couple of months ago. But for now, she had a challenge on her hands, and she needed to focus on that.

She watched Emilio walking toward the guesthouse with his nieces trudging beside him. She could tell from his troubled expression that he didn't know how things were going to go. Didn't know if staying at the guesthouse for the summer was going to work.

But Kitty needed him here. For Mason's sake, she *had* to make it work.

As Emilio carried suitcases and boxes into the guesthouse and set them in the ground-floor suite of rooms that would be theirs for the summer, one question hammered at him. Was this the right move?

His life had done a complete turn-around. Rather than deciding whether to buy Steelers season tickets or pondering his next career move, his entire goal now was to raise his nieces well.

But could he do it? He barely knew them. Being the gift-bearing uncle home for a week's leave was way different from being, basically, a father. And Nora, in particular, was a handful.

Having plied the girls with cookies, Kitty was showing them around the suite, chatting cheerfully. She seemed to be connecting with them a little, so when Emilio went outside to get the last load, he allowed himself to pause and take a breath.

He looked out over the river that had been such an important part of his childhood. The sun was setting behind the trees on the other bank, and a cool breeze rippled the water. A family of ducks swam downstream, quacking.

It was a different world from the city where the girls had grown up, but if anything could help them heal, it was this place. He'd seen the wonder in Nora's eyes when she'd spotted the deer. He'd never seen an expression like that on her face before, and he wanted to see more of it. If staying here this summer worked out for them, he was prepared to make a permanent home in River Haven.

He breathed in the fresh, country air and then went inside and set down the last load of boxes.

Mr. Wright, Kitty's father, was in the suite now, showing Alice an old wooden rocking horse he'd cleaned up and brought in for her. Emilio greeted the older man and shook his hand. Mr. Wright had always been good to Emilio, sympathetic to a child growing up without a father. The man had aged quite a bit, no doubt in part because he'd lost his beloved wife. But he looked strong, and Alice was already staring up at him with something like adoration. She was a kid who lacked male role models, just as he had been.

Then Emilio noticed a boy of about nine, close by Kitty's side. He was looking up at her pleadingly. "Can I go ride bikes, Mom? Liam and his cousin are outside."

"Say hello to my friend first," she said. "Emilio, this is my son, Mason. Mason, this is Nora and Alice's uncle, Emilio."

"Pleased to meet you," the boy mumbled. When Emilio held out his hand, Mason shook it. Then he looked at Kitty. "Can I go, Mom?"

"Be careful and stay on this side of the park," she said. She dropped a kiss on his head, the love she held for her son plain in the smile on her face.

That was something Emilio hadn't seen: his old friend Kitty as a mother. The role suited her.

Mason stopped at the doorway and turned back. "Want to come, Nora?" he asked politely.

Kitty smiled her approval at him. The boy had obviously been raised well. Just as obviously, he would rather this strange-looking older girl didn't join him, so it was doubly admirable that he'd had the grace to invite her.

"I hate bikes," Nora said, her lip curling.

"Okay. See ya." The little boy shrugged and ran off.

Emilio opened his mouth to ask Nora if she'd ever actually ridden a bike, but then stopped himself. He was pretty sure she hadn't, and he didn't want to make her lose face.

"There's lots else to do around here in the summer," Kitty said. "Boating, swimming, sports leagues. And the library has a bunch of activities for young people."

"And there's fishing," Emilio interjected. "Remember when I tried to scare you with a handful of worms, Kitty?"

Nora made a face. "You *did* that?"

"He didn't get away with it." Kitty was laughing, her whole face lighting up with the memory. "I pushed him into the river."

Nora snorted out a laugh, the first he'd heard from her today. Score one for Kitty.

She had said he wasn't her type. Just as well. But there had been a time, way back, when he'd developed a major crush on her. That was before he'd known that she wasn't for him. That serious relationships weren't for him. Given his family, he wasn't going to risk anything but short, superficial relationships, and Kitty deserved way more than that.

She raised an eyebrow, and he realized he was staring at her. He cleared his throat. "Is your brother around?" He'd heard that Kitty's older brother lived in the guesthouse, too.

"No, he and his fiancée and her kids left early this morning. They headed up to Cook Forest for a week with another family. They're camping."

"Ugh," said Nora. "I hate camping."

Emilio was pretty sure his nieces had never been camping.

He blew out a breath. He felt inept with his nieces, and especially awkward with Nora. Alice he could just pick up and toss in the air and make her giggle. She was easy and cute, if a little insecure. But Nora? She was a tougher case.

Suddenly, a black and white kitten ran

through the room, chased by a chubby calico.

"Kitties!" Alice cried rapturously. She started to run after them.

"Wait," Emilio called. "You can't run all around the guesthouse without—" He trailed off, because Alice was already out of earshot.

Nora headed after her sister. "I'll watch out for her," she said to the adults.

"Your girls are welcome anywhere in the place," Mr. Wright said. "But I'll follow along, make sure they don't get lost. Good to see you again, Emilio."

Alone in the suite with Kitty, Emilio sank into a chair. "I'm in way over my head," he told her. "Alice cries a lot, and Nora's a big grouch. I don't know what to do with them when they get upset, which is a lot of the time."

Kitty perched on the arm of the couch. "Yeah," she said. "Twelve and two. Some really emotional ages. Maybe especially for girls."

"Girls whose mother basically abandoned them."

"So…you ended up getting permanent custody?" Kitty's voice was kind, gentle.

"Yeah. Just had the final hearing a month ago." And his sister, Bianca, hadn't called or contacted the girls since. He let his head sink into his hands, then lifted it and looked at her. "Did I make a mistake?"

"You mean by bringing them here?"

"By thinking I could be a good guardian for them. I don't know…maybe they would do better with experienced foster parents?"

"No, Emilio." Kitty slid off the arm of the couch and knelt in front of him. "They need you, and you can do it. I'll help you every step of the way. I'm a good teacher, remember?"

He did remember, and it made him smile. He'd been a math guy, never too good with words and writing, and Kitty had coached him through high school English classes.

"You're a good teacher, but I wasn't a very good student," he said.

"You passed, didn't you?"

"I did," he admitted. "I even like to read now."

"See?" she said triumphantly. "You can learn."

She met his eyes, and for just a moment, he couldn't look away. It wasn't just the beauty of her striking violet eyes. It was the faith that shone out from them. Kitty genuinely believed in him. He hadn't known how much he needed that vote of confidence until he saw it in her eyes.

He blew out a breath, stood and started unpacking a box. He definitely didn't need to be getting all soft and mushy around Kitty. "I really appreciate your taking us in like this," he said.

"It's not like you're doing nothing in exchange," she said. "I'm counting on you to help me make the Fourth of July celebration a big success."

"I'll do what I can." Even though fireworks freaked him out. Which he hadn't found the opportunity to tell her.

It was going to be an interesting summer.

Chapter Two

On Monday afternoon, Kitty hurried home, conscious of new responsibilities, and changed into shorts and a T-shirt. Mason was already home from school, skipping rocks on the river. She called for him to join her and headed next door to the guesthouse.

Her father was busy chatting with a couple of guests, so Kitty looked around for Emilio and his family. Not finding them indoors or out, she tapped on the door of their suite.

Emilio answered, looking frazzled. Competing sounds of a children's TV show and hard-driving music came from behind him.

"Hi! Mason and I are going to walk down to the park. Would you all want to join us? Maybe you and I could talk a little bit about a schedule for working on the Fourth of July event. And the kids could see the town and get some fresh air."

"We would definitely like to get out of here," Emilio said, turning to look back into the suite. "Right, girls?"

There was no answer.

"By 'we' I mean 'I,'" he added ruefully.

"Should I leave you to get them going, or would you like Mason and me to try to motivate them?" She wouldn't have even asked, except that she hated to see Emilio looking so careworn. She'd promised that she would help him figure out parenting, and now seemed like a good time to start.

Emilio stepped back from the door and gestured for them to come in. "I don't seem to be real successful at getting them to do anything, so if you want to give it a try, I would welcome that."

Kitty patted Mason's shoulder. "Why don't you see if you can get Alice excited about coming to the park?" she said. "I'll talk to Nora." Kitty had purposely given herself the harder job. She had no illusions that Nora would be thrilled to join in a family outing. Even if she did want to go, it was doubtful that she would admit it. But Kitty had a few tricks up her sleeve for dealing with kids of Nora's age. She just had to figure out which one to pull out first.

As she walked past Emilio, she couldn't help noticing that the suite was strewn with boxes, clothes and toys.

"Sorry, it's a mess. I've been doing some work for my online class." He was taking classes via his veteran's benefits, Kitty knew that. If he was able to think with two noisy kids in a small suite, her hat was off to him.

Emilio ran his fingers through his hair, making it stand on end. "Don't worry, I'll clean up as soon as we get settled."

"No judgment from me. Kids equal messes, always." She put a reassuring arm around him and was surprised when he leaned in. Weirdly enough, it was hard to step away. *It's Emilio,* she reminded herself. She must have missed her old friend more than she'd realized.

Mason squatted beside Alice, who sat on the floor in front of the TV, an old blanket cuddled to her cheek, her thumb in her mouth. "Want to go to the park?" he asked her. "There's a teeter-totter. And swings."

Alice tilted her head to one side. "Nora go?"

Aha, Kitty thought, *a way in.* She headed to the open bedroom door through which Nora's music blared. She tapped on the edge of the door, once quietly, then again more loudly. When there was no response, she went in and waved her hands until Nora looked up from her old-fashioned-looking iPad.

Kitty mimed turning the music down, and Nora did, frowning.

"Thanks," Kitty said, smiling at the girl. "Mason and I are headed for the park, and Alice wants to go along. But I don't think she'll go without you. Would you be willing to join us?"

Nora narrowed her eyes and scowled. She looked down at her T-shirt and leggings.

Kitty read her mind easily, experienced as she was with middle school girls. Nora was concerned about what to wear. Possibly, she felt too lazy to change out of her rot-in-bed clothes. Or, more likely, she didn't want to show up in a new place dressed wrong.

If that was the case, a clothes-shopping trip might be needed. Based on what Kitty had seen of yesterday's outfit, Nora's clothes were more suited to a sophisticated city than a small town.

For now, the goal was to get Nora and Alice—and Emilio—out of the house. "You might want to wear some shorts. It's hot out," she said. "Or jeans, if you'd rather. Something you don't mind getting dirty." Then she went out to the front room. Mason sat on the floor beside Alice, seemingly engrossed in the kids' show that Alice was watching.

Emilio was closing his laptop. "Any success?" he asked.

"She's coming. Just give her a minute to change her clothes. Mason, Alice, come on, let's go."

A few minutes later, they were walking the couple of blocks to the town park. Mason had taken Alice's hand and was talking a mile a minute about the park and what he wanted to do there during the summer. Silently, Kitty thanked God for her kind, compassionate son. He'd sensed that Alice needed cheering up and was trying to help her feel better.

Nora trailed along behind the two younger kids, hands thrust into the pockets of her ripped black jeans.

Kitty and Emilio walked behind them, more slowly. Kitty's goal was to pin down a working schedule with Emilio, but she sensed he needed a little time to decompress before he started making plans with her.

"What did you do all day?" she asked him.

He blew out a sigh and shook his head. "Not much," he said. "We did pick up some workbooks for Nora to go through this summer."

"Her idea or yours?"

"Both. She…has some catching up to do. Her environment wasn't conducive to concentrating on her studies."

"It's great she's willing to do schoolwork in the summer," she told him. "All subjects?"

"English is hardest for her," he said. "Sound familiar?"

Emilio had failed an English class early in high school, which was what had led to Kitty tutoring him.

"If she needs help, I'm glad to work with her. That's what I teach." Tutoring might be a way to build a connection with the girl. "How about Alice? What did she do all day?"

"Mostly she watched TV. She didn't seem to mind. I guess that's what she's used to doing. But I don't like the idea of her spending the whole summer that way."

Kitty wasn't a fan of lots of screen time for kids, but she also knew TV could be a necessary babysitter. "I'm sure you'll find her better things to do once you're settled in."

Around them, the street was waking up from its midday silence. Kids were home from school and playing in yards. A couple of older gentlemen were strolling, and two moms lingered at a bus stop, talking and laughing, enjoying the summery breeze.

As they got closer to the park, Mason and Alice ran toward the small play area. Nora trudged behind them.

"I haven't been a total dud all day," Emilio said, his tone apologetic. "I did convince them to play by the river for a little while, when we saw some ducks down there. And I grilled them lunch, and we grocery shopped."

"That sounds great! I'm impressed you got that much done."

"Yeah, well, don't be too impressed. I should have figured this stuff out beforehand. I didn't really think about how I was going to entertain them here."

"It'll take time," Kitty reassured him. "School's out at the end of the week, and then summer programs will start up. Maybe we can find a camp for Nora for a week or two."

"Camp?" Emilio shook his head. "Not yet. I want to keep both girls close for now. No matter how grouchy or whiny they get, they need to know I'm with them and here for them. They need to see me, day in and day out."

Kitty's heart melted a little. Emilio so obviously cared for his nieces. "That sounds smart. But there are camps for kids that are really just day programs, some a week long or a couple days a week for a few weeks. I'll ask around and see what options other kids are doing. Maybe I could even find a couple of nice girls Nora's age that might kind of take her under their wings."

Emilio looked skeptical. "Nora won't go under anyone's wing. She's had to be the mama bird most of her life. Even before Alice, I think Nora took care of her mom half the time. And she's cared for Alice her whole life."

Kitty's heart went out to the family. "That can change. She needs friends her age."

"True, you're right." He hesitated. "You know so much more about kids. I suspect, though, that Nora needs to choose friends herself and feel compatible with them. Not have them assigned to her."

He was right. "That's fair. If you want, I'll just find out what programs and activities some of the more pleasant girls are doing and we'll see if Nora can join the same ones. Let twelve-year-old nature take its course."

The lines between Emilio's thick eyebrows were already softening. "That would be great, if we can get Nora involved in some positive things." He grimaced. "Maybe she'll stop playing her music so loud."

That was a problem Kitty understood. "You know, there are fancy headphones the kids like. They're expensive, but I'd guess if you would spring for a pair for Nora, she might use them instead of blaring her music. Because if there are other guests in the guesthouse, we might have to ask her to turn it down anyway."

"Great idea." Emilio put an arm around her and gave her a side hug. "You are a genius. I really do appreciate your help with this."

His praise warmed her almost as much as his comforting arm around her shoulder.

They'd reached the park now. As they talked, they strolled slowly toward the swings and slides where the three kids were playing—or, in Nora's case, standing.

"I still need to figure out how to keep

Alice from watching TV all day," he said. "Maybe I'm a bad person, but I just can't play dolls with her for hours at a stretch."

Kitty shrugged. "Kids are better off playing with kids, I think. Maybe you would want to get Alice started with child-care or a sitter a couple hours each day. She could get used to it and meet some kids for playdates. You need time for your own studies, right?"

"I'm taking one course, but I do need to get her accustomed to some kind of child-care when I start full-time in the fall."

"Wow, good for you." Kitty was impressed by the grown-up version of Emilio. He was way more focused than he'd been back in high school. "What are you majoring in?"

"I haven't 100 percent decided," he said. "The logical field for someone with my background would be criminal justice or something security-related, but actually…" He trailed off, a flush coloring his cheekbones.

"What?" she asked, fascinated. "Tell me!"

"I'm thinking about getting a degree in counseling. I got so much help from the counselors at the VA, and I think it would be cool to do what they're doing."

Kitty blinked. Obviously, there were things she didn't know about her old friend. Emilio seemed so together, and he'd had so much success in his military career. She would never have thought of him as someone who needed counseling.

"I also want to find some part-time work for myself," he said. "Ideally something related to mental health, but I'm not sure what options there are."

Kitty opened her mouth to start making suggestions, but he waved his hand.

"Don't you worry about me," he said. "If you can help my nieces, that would be amazing. But I've got to figure out my life for myself."

"Sorry, sorry," she said, laughing. "It's the teacher in me. I want to solve everybody's problems."

"I hope that's not a problem that's happening over on the playground," he said.

Expecting to see Nora being rude to other girls, or Alice crying, Kitty looked toward the playground and saw that Mason was yelling at another boy. They looked ready to come to blows.

Before Kitty and Emilio could reach the pair of angry boys, Nora strode over to them. She stood beside Mason and glared at the boy, who gave her a dubious look and ran away. Nora did indeed look threatening in her work boots and heavy makeup.

But Kitty's concern was that the kid who'd been arguing with Mason was the same one who had teased him about his father's bad-conduct discharge. Had he been badgering Mason again? If so, that made it more important than ever that she get the Fourth of July event into shape as a way to show that she and Mason were patriotic.

Emilio would be a big help with that, given his heroic background in military service. But right now, he was preoccupied with his nieces. She hoped that situation could get figured out so that she could start working with him to make the Fourth of July event a huge success.

Emilio followed Kitty, who was marching toward the play area. She had the air of a cavalry officer rushing to the rescue. He could have told her that wasn't how modern warfare worked, but she didn't seem to be in any mood to listen.

"What happened?" she demanded of her son. "Was he teasing you again?"

"It's fine, Mom," Mason said, sounding irritated.

Emilio caught a glimpse of the other boy, now across the playground, making some kind of gesture toward Mason.

Nora must have seen it, too. She turned toward the kid and made a gesture of her own, one that was blocked from Emilio's view. The other kid's jaw dropped. He turned away and hurried toward a woman who must be his mother.

Emilio walked toward Nora, who glanced

at him and then away, her shoulders hunching a little.

"It was kind of you to help Mason," he said.

Nora looked up at him, her eyes searching, like she was waiting for the other shoe to drop. There was a tiny spark in her eyes, as if his praise meant something to her. A moment later, her habitual sneer was back, but Emilio felt like he might have made a tiny connection.

He was glad to know that Nora was the type who would stand up for another kid. That was something he needed to focus on—not her recalcitrance, not her weird outfits, but her strength and her desire to help those younger or weaker than she was.

Nora lifted Alice into one of the swings and started pushing her. Mason was climbing on the old-fashioned monkey bars.

"What was that all about?" Emilio asked Kitty.

Kitty frowned. "Mason has started getting teased about his father," she said.

"Your ex? Why?"

She sighed. "When we lived here together, he made a big deal out of being a military hero. He even spoke at some events. But as I found out a year ago, he actually was no hero. He got a bad-conduct discharge."

Emilio whistled. Those weren't given out for minor infractions. "That's serious. What did he do?"

"He never would tell me the whole story, but I know he was drinking on the job and some other soldiers were put at risk by what he did."

Anger tightened Emilio's fists, but he tried to focus on what it meant to Kitty. "So…he was lying to you as well?"

Kitty blew out a disgusted breath. "Yeah, about that and a lot of other stuff. Mason and I are well out of that marriage—not that I'm a fan of divorce—but there were just a lot of ways Jeff was harming us. Anyway, someone spread the news about the bad-conduct discharge, and a couple of boys started teasing Mason about it.

Saying his dad was a liar, calling it stolen valor. All of which is true, unfortunately."

"That's rough."

"So I can't tell Mason to tell them to look up the truth, because the truth is exactly what they say. That's why I came up with the idea of running the Fourth of July celebration. I want to make it really great. Having our family involved in that will help show that we're good, patriotic Americans and that we didn't know about the lies my ex was telling."

Emilio listened to this tirade, frowning. He could see from Kitty's red face and the tension in her body that it was very serious to her.

"What?" she demanded. She had always been able to tell when he didn't agree with what she was saying.

"It's just, you can't always fix what people think. Your character and Mason's character will win out in the end, but you can't force people to believe you're patriotic. And beyond that, you can't fix conflict between a couple of boys Mason's age. They'll work it out."

Kitty propped a hand on her hip and frowned at him. Emilio had to force himself not to smile, because the truth was, she looked adorable. As if she might stamp her foot any minute.

"I can fix it," she said firmly. "And I'll figure out a way to do it. But you have to help. Help me make this Fourth of July celebration great."

"I'm glad to work on it with you," he said mildly. "It's a good cause." He was telling the truth. It was a good cause… even if Kitty was wrong about what she thought it would achieve in the minds of the townspeople.

The kids played a little longer, but things were going downhill. Mason looked depressed, Nora wore her habitual scowl, and Alice was fussy, probably in need of the nap she hadn't gotten. So when Mr. Wright came striding across the park, holding a sheaf of paper in his hands, Emilio was happy for the distraction.

"Hey, folks," the older man said. "Anyone interested in dinner at The Hungry Hubcap? We can take it out or eat in. I brought menus." He waved the papers and looked at Emilio. "We only have one other family of guests this week—at least until Friday—but they're using the kitchen to make a family dinner. That's the excuse I needed not to cook. Sound good?"

"Sounds great," Emilio said. He wasn't much of a cook, himself.

Mr. Wright knelt down and showed a kids' menu to Alice. There were food items to color in and menu offerings printed on the side.

Mason came over and squatted down beside Alice. "Their chicken nuggets are great."

"Nuggets!" Alice smiled up at Mr. Wright, then at Mason. She was loving the attention she was getting here, and it warmed Emilio's heart. It made him glad he'd decided to come to River Haven.

Mr. Wright glanced over at Nora. "Kids' menu or adult menu?"

She rolled her eyes, but at least she turned away from the older man to do it. "Adult," she said.

Kitty told Nora a little about the restaurant. She waved to another girl about Nora's age who was walking by, and Emilio could read her well enough to know she was debating whether to call the girl over. But she decided not to, which was probably best. Nora took any interference in her life as a challenge to her independence.

As they all left the park together, Emilio felt like a weight had lifted off of him. He needed help to raise his nieces well, and he was hoping—and starting to believe— he'd come to the right place.

Chapter Three

Kitty was tired the next day after school. Her students had been wild because it was the last week of classes, and she'd had trouble sleeping the night before, thinking about what Emilio had said.

He didn't think it was possible for her to fix the disaster that her ex had caused. He'd said you couldn't change what people thought of you, and that her and Mason's reputations would improve naturally.

But Kitty wasn't the type to let things take their course. She couldn't stand to see Mason treated badly or suffer consequences of his father's mistake. He deserved better, and she was going to make it happen for him. If she managed a terrific, super-patriotic celebration, and Mason was involved, it would be the visual aid the town needed to disassociate them completely from her ex's bad conduct.

It was a rainy Tuesday evening, and although she would have liked to laze on the couch, she needed to pick up a couple of books at the library. On impulse, she decided to invite Nora to come along. Not just because helping Nora would get Emilio even more committed to helping with the Fourth of July celebration. That was part of it, but she also felt for the lonely, bored almost-teenager.

Nora's sigh and eye roll made it obvious she didn't want to go, but Emilio insisted, and she grumpily agreed. They decided to walk—Kitty needed the exercise, and she was guessing fresh air would be good for Nora, too—and Emilio offered to come pick them up later. The library was only six blocks away, but it looked like the rain might get worse by the time they were ready to leave.

As they approached the library, Nora stopped walking and stared. "That's *it*?" Nora asked, genuine surprise in her tone.

"Uh-huh. That's it." Kitty looked at their little town library with new eyes. It was a small, squat building, unassuming on the outside, not particularly impressive. "They have a great collection of books and DVDs, and some fun programs. You'll see."

They went down the stairs to the library, and there was Gemma, Kitty's good friend and their neighbor, working at the desk. She was petite, with dark hair buzzed short on one side and long on the other. She wore a bright pink dress in a vintage style that suited her.

Nora scanned the library, clearly unimpressed. The large main area held adult books, DVDs and a bank of not-so-new computers. Displays of Fourth of July books and videos flanked the circulation desk, one featuring kids' items and the other featuring adult ones.

The library was relatively busy, with several people using the computers and more browsing the shelves. The sound of kids' voices came from the room that adjoined the main one.

"You're used to something bigger?" Kitty asked Nora.

"Yeah, the library back home was like ten times this big. Not that I'm a big fan of libraries." Nora shifted from foot to foot, as if she wanted to be anywhere but here.

Kitty didn't let herself get discouraged. Nora's too-cool-for-school attitude was one she dealt with on a daily basis in her work as a middle school teacher. Plus, Mason wasn't an enthusiastic reader and had been glad she'd let him stay home tonight, watching a game with his grandfather. But Kitty believed in the power of books and libraries. "Let's just give it a try."

When they approached the desk, Gemma

greeted them cheerfully, and Kitty introduced Nora.

"It's great to meet you," she said with her characteristic enthusiasm. "I'm in charge of programming for kids and teens. I'm super excited about the first summer teen program that's coming up next week. We're going to make terrariums!"

Nora lifted an eyebrow. "What's a terrarium?"

"Oh, they're so cool." Gemma looked through her phone and pulled up a picture of a round glass globe with succulents inside and layers of pretty dirt and stones.

"Nice," Nora said in a voice that clearly meant the opposite.

"Oh no." Gemma's face fell. "Is it a bad idea? How can I make it better?"

Nora lifted her hands and shrugged.

In a flash, Kitty remembered that Nora was moved by other people's problems. She took care of her sister in a nurturing way, and she'd stepped in when Mason was being teased. "Gemma is new in her job," Kitty explained to Nora. "She's really hoping to make it a success."

"Yeah, and you're the first teenager I've told about it, so your reaction is freaking me out."

Something like compassion came into Nora's eyes. "I'm sorry," she said. "They actually look pretty cool. I'm just upset to be away from my sister."

"Wow," Gemma said. "When I was your age, I wanted to be away from my sister as much as possible."

"Alice needs me." Nora's words were simple, sad and sweet.

"Your uncle will take good care of her," Kitty said, "and you can be back before she goes to bed."

"So can I sign you up for the terrarium program?" Gemma asked. "Please sign up. That blank page isn't going to appeal to anyone."

"Sure, okay," Nora said.

While Nora filled out the signup sheet, Kitty checked out the books she'd had on hold. Then she spotted a girl she knew browsing the young adult books. Izzy was a nice girl and might be the perfect friend to help Nora adjust her attitude. But, mindful of Emilio's idea that Nora would want to choose her own friends, Kitty forced herself to be low-key about it. She walked over to Izzy. "Finding anything good?"

"Oh hi, Ms. MacIntyre. Yeah, I'm checking out the fantasy books. I need a new series to binge for the summer."

"If you need suggestions, Gemma, the new librarian, could probably help." She gestured toward the circulation desk, where Nora and Gemma were finishing up.

"Maybe I'll ask her what's good," Izzy said. "She seems nice."

After Nora and Gemma had finished talking, Kitty beckoned to her. Sure, Emilio wanted Nora to pick her own friends, but given Nora's reserve, that could take all summer. She wanted to give the girl a nudge, and Izzy was just the kind of sweet person who might look past Nora's rough exterior to her kind heart.

Nora walked across the library, her expression guarded.

Kitty gestured to her former student. "This is Izzy. She was in my class last year, and she's looking for something to cure her summer boredom. Izzy, this is Nora, who just moved to town. I wanted you guys to meet."

Nora looked at the thick volumes in Izzy's hands. "*That's* your solution to boredom?" she asked.

From the other side of the big bookshelf came a snicker, and then Izzy's twin, Ishmael, sauntered over. Ishmael was a good kid and smart, but a little awkward because he'd experienced his growth spurt early. He was big and tall and had the beginnings of facial hair. Beside him, most of the other seventh-grade boys looked like little kids.

Kitty introduced Nora to Ishmael. "What are you doing to stay intellectually active this summer?" she asked the boy, softening her lofty words with a smile to show she was half kidding.

"I'm bingeing TV shows and Cheetos," he said, and Nora high-fived him. Izzy rolled her eyes.

Oh, well. If Nora could connect with either one of the twins, it might be a good start.

Across the library, she spotted the father of the bully who had been teasing Mason. He'd returned to town from a deployment about six months ago, and although Kitty had seen him, she hadn't had the chance to meet him. "I'll be right back," she said to Nora. She walked over and introduced herself.

The man's eyes widened. "So you're the wife of the faker."

"Ex-wife," she corrected. Why couldn't people get that she wasn't with Jeff anymore? She almost wished she were dating someone else, as a few friends were urging her to do. Maybe that would stop people from associating her with her ex.

She'd heard the man was a little combative, so she deliberately kept her voice low and calm. "Look, I'm not going to try to make excuses for my ex. He did some bad things, but your son has been teasing my son about it. It's not Mason's fault that his dad made stuff up about his military service."

The man looked skeptical.

"You want your kid to be responsible for everything you do?" she challenged him, still keeping her tone friendly.

He frowned. "Yeah, you're right, but it burns me. Some of us risked our lives—some still are—and your ex-husband tries to steal the glory."

"I get it," Kitty said, cringing again at what her husband had done. "I was very upset to learn about it, believe me. But it all happened before he and I met. By the time I learned about it, I'd married him and we had a son. There's no way I can change what he did, and there's certainly nothing Mason can do about his dad's past behavior."

The door to the library opened, and Emilio came in, Alice on his hip.

Kitty's heart lifted just seeing him. He was so sensitive and kind, despite the difficult and sometimes violent work he'd done in the service.

Emilio smiled at her, glanced at the bully's dad and raised an eyebrow. Then he scanned the room. His expression darkened.

What was bothering him? Kitty looked over to see that Nora was laughing up at Ishmael. They were both looking at a graphic novel. Izzy was nowhere in sight.

"Nora," Emilio said sharply and a little too loud for a public place, "come on, it's time to go."

Nora looked at Ishmael with a wry expression, and they exchanged words in a low voice. Then she meandered over to her uncle.

"We'll be in the car," Emilio said to Kitty. He ushered Nora out, anger in every line of his body.

Kitty said goodbye to the bully's dad

and followed. This was *not* what she'd had in mind when she'd brought Nora here. She'd hoped to show Emilio that she could be a real help. Instead, she'd made him angry. And his overbearing behavior had no doubt annoyed Nora.

It looked like she was about to have an interesting conversation.

Emilio was angry, but he didn't want to get into an argument with Kitty in front of his niece. So their ride home from the library was silent, and by mutual agreement, they separated to get their kids into bed. They'd meet outside later.

Emilio needed the time. He needed to cool off. Needed to get perspective on his emotions and what he'd seen.

It didn't help that he'd finally gotten a text from his sister. She was in Arizona with her new boyfriend, and they were having a great time. She didn't know when—or if—she'd be back in Pennsylvania.

She hadn't even asked about the girls.

He was angry at his sister, and worried, too. He wanted to raise his nieces well, which could mean a lot of different things. But one thing it for sure meant was keeping them safe.

Nora was at a dangerous age. To him, she looked and acted like a child. But children grew up fast these days. Nora had seen more than she should have of the seedier, adult side of life.

He wanted her to have a childhood, not move too quickly into boys and dating and all the things that went along with that. It was what his sister had done, and look at the outcome. She was flighty and uncaring about her daughters.

On top of that, Emilio was a bachelor uncle and had no idea of how to address the issues of a young girl becoming a woman.

Which was why he'd been so upset to see Nora giggling with an older boy.

A broad, grassy lawn sloped down from the guesthouse to the river. He found a double wooden swing and sat, facing the river. The air was fragrant with the rich smell of dirt and plants and river, cool after the earlier rainstorm they'd had. He took deep breaths and felt some of the tightness in his shoulders relax.

"Hey," Kitty said, appearing at the side of the swing. She glanced at the seat, then at him, and then sat down.

At which point Emilio realized that the double swing didn't give a whole lot of individual room.

But that didn't matter. This was his good friend Kitty, and the air was cool. "Don't you want a jacket?" he asked her.

"I forgot it was cold," she said. "I'll be okay."

He put an arm around her, giving her a quick side hug. "I'm known for being a furnace," he said. "You just let me know if you get cold, and we'll warm you up."

Inside, he cringed. Had that sounded like a come-on? He was really only con-cerned about his friend's comfort, not wanting her to be cold. That was all he was thinking about. All he *could* think about.

"So, let's talk this through," she said. "What was upsetting you at the library?"

He glanced over at her. "You're kidding, right? Nora needs to be supervised better."

She raised an eyebrow. "Hello? I was right across the room from them. And I know the kid she was talking to. He's a nice guy."

His shoulders tightened up again. "Nora is twelve. She doesn't need to be meeting older boys, no matter how nice."

Inside, he added, *and you don't need to get distracted by some guy, yourself.* Seeing Kitty talking to that jarhead was what had set him off in the first place—not that he was going to admit it.

"You're being unreasonable," she said. "Ishmael could be a good friend to Nora. So could his twin sister, Izzy."

"That kid had more than friendship on his mind," Emilio said automatically, even though he wasn't sure whether that was true.

"No, he didn't. He may look grown-up, but he's still a child, the same age as Nora. Boys and girls can be friends without it being romantic. Look at us."

"Maybe." Emilio knew he sounded grumpy.

Inside, he was considering what she had said.

Look at us.

He appreciated Kitty's sparkling eyes and enjoyed her spunk. She stood right up to him. He'd never liked the type of woman who agreed with everything you said, or pretended to. He knew he could get overbearing, could run right over a meek, overly agreeable woman. He needed someone who would call him on his mistakes.

Their eyes met and held for a longer time than was quite comfortable. The chirp of crickets rose and fell, mingled with the lapping sound of the river against the dock.

"Look, Emilio," she said.

"I'm sorry," he started at the same time.

They both smiled. "You first," he insisted.

"Okay." She turned a little to look at him head on. "I'm not gonna do everything right with Nora and Alice. If I was wrong letting Nora talk with Ishmael… well, I *wasn't* wrong, but I'll give it some thought." She smiled, her mouth quirking up more on one side than the other.

"Thanks. I'll think on it, too."

She drew in a breath and let it out slowly. "And… I did listen to what you said last night. Maybe I'm wrong to put so much stock in making this Fourth of July thing great, too, but… I really want to try. For Mason's sake. Are you in?"

He didn't hesitate. "One hundred percent."

Their eyes met again.

Was there anything he *wouldn't* do for Kitty?

Warning bells rang in the back of Emilio's head, starting low and getting louder. He needed to focus on his goal of raising his nieces well. Needed to remember that romantic love ruined everything.

He stood, making the bench rock and jangle. "I'm going in," he said. He walked away, knowing he had been awkward and abrupt.

But all his instincts told him that he was in a danger zone. That had been a close call, and he had to get out of it however he could.

Chapter Four

On Saturday morning after breakfast, Kitty went outside with Mason, doing a little happy dance. "School's out! Woohoo! School's out!" She loved her job, but she also loved having summers off.

"Yaay!" Mason turned a cartwheel with more enthusiasm than skill.

It was a perfect June day—cool now, with no humidity, and bright sunshine that promised to be hot by afternoon. The air smelled fresh, and the grass and trees were a lush, early-summer shade of green.

Over at the guesthouse, a young couple emerged, looking starstruck with each other as they strolled hand in hand. They must be the honeymooners Kitty's father had mentioned. A family of four, two adults and two school-aged kids, pulled bikes from the back of their pickup and headed toward the bike trail across the river.

And then Emilio came out, holding Alice in one arm. Nora followed slowly, looking at her tablet, and the three came over toward Kitty and Mason.

"Guess what," Mason said. "My mom said we can go to the lake this afternoon!"

Alice smiled and nodded. "Okay."

"*If* you get your chores done," Kitty reminded Mason.

Nora looked up. "We don't have chores," she said.

"Wish I didn't!" Mason made a face and then trudged over toward the garden Kitty had assigned him to weed today.

Kitty watched him fondly. He was such a good kid. He groused like anybody else about chores, but he was a hard worker and a big help to her. "I have to do my chores this morning, too. My house isn't going to clean itself."

Alice and Nora wandered over to where Mason was and stood watching him as he pulled weeds.

Emilio frowned. "My nieces should have chores, too, shouldn't they?"

She nodded. "Yeah, probably. Alice could pick up her toys. Nora could do a lot more, but you have to make her."

"How?"

Kitty frowned. "Just tell her to do it. If she says no, well, then she loses a privilege."

"Like going to the lake?" He hesitated. "That is, if we're invited. It's fine if you want to have a day alone with your son."

"You're invited," she said quickly. She hadn't given it much thought, but she did want them to come, even though the idea of it gave her a funny kind of quiver inside.

She shoved that feeling aside. "As far as making her do chores, you don't want to give her a punishment that's going to be a punishment to you. So don't tell her she has to stay home from the lake if she doesn't do her chores—not if that would mean you and Alice have to stay home, too."

"Good point," Emilio said.

"Maybe you could take her tablet away if she won't do her chores. Or you could take the positive approach and let her earn money toward getting a phone. That's something all the kids want."

Emilio grimaced. "When I was growing up, Mom always said, 'Them that don't work, don't eat.'"

Kitty laughed. "My parents said something similar, but these are different times." She looked thoughtfully at Nora, who was kneeling to re-tie Alice's little sneaker. "You could also ask her to help or supervise Alice in her chores and remind her she needs to be a good role model. She seems to have a caring heart, especially for her sister."

Emilio smiled. "I'm glad you can see beneath the crusty exterior. Maybe you can even give me tips on getting her to wear some better clothes."

Kitty laughed. Today, Nora was wearing a pair of tight black leggings and a long gray hoodie with the name of a band on the back of it. She had to be sweating in the heavy clothes, but the look was consistent with her usual style.

"I mean, black every single day?" Emilio said.

"Hey, her hoodie is gray, not black." Kitty laughed. "Choose your battles, my friend. If she does her chores, it doesn't matter what she wears. And her style might evolve if you leave her alone about it."

Emilio looked relieved. "I've been hands-off about it so far, but I've wondered if that was right. Especially moving here, where people dress a little more traditionally."

"Hands-off is fine," she said. "Mason went through a phase of wearing all camo, all the time. I didn't love it, but it was the least of my worries… And, amazingly, it all went away, and now he dresses nor-mally."

"Okay, girls," Emilio called to his nieces. "We've got our own chores to do. Let's get busy."

"Aw, man!" Nora's tone echoed the tone Mason had used, but Kitty thought she de-tected a little pleasure, too. Maybe Nora wanted to have chores like Mason did. Like most kids did. Maybe she wanted a normal life, contributing to her family by doing a few kid-appropriate chores rather than by being put in charge of too much too early.

Kitty watched the three of them walk into the guesthouse together, the sound of Emilio's reasonable voice drifting back toward her.

He was such a good guy. Last night, when they sat together on the swing, she had felt so warm and close to him. Almost a little more than just friends.

It was weird how abruptly he had left, but maybe he'd felt uncomfortable with the vibe, too.

Regardless, it was nice having him here, if a little more intense than she'd expected. Maybe anyone at their age and stage would have a few too many long looks. Maybe both of them had been single too long.

Although she'd only been single for a year. She didn't have any excuse for mooning at Emilio, her old friend.

The door of the guesthouse opened, and her father came out, wearing work clothes that indicated he was on the way to the family auto repair shop next door. Its operations were limited while her brother was away, but Dad would keep things going along.

Dad reached her and looked over his shoulder. "Nice having those folks here," he said, gesturing in the direction Emilio and his nieces had gone. "They'll fit right in. That Alice is a sweetie."

"She is," Kitty said.

"I miss your brother and little Rylee," he said. Rylee was the younger child of Summer, her soon-to-be sister-in-law. Dad had formed a special bond with the little girl.

"I miss them, too," she said. "I'm so glad Jake and Summer are getting married and settling right down the road. The wedding will be here before we know it."

"Just three weeks," he said. Then he looked at her. "What about you getting married again? Any thoughts on that?"

Kitty reeled back a little, looking at her father. "You know I don't have any interest," she said. "I was burned."

"You were, and I feel terrible about that. But don't close your mind to love."

Kitty watched a couple of bunnies nibbling on the grass at the edge of the garden. Then she looked at her father again. "What brought this on?"

He looked back at the guesthouse. "Oh, just thinking."

Kitty narrowed her eyes. "Thinking about what?"

He smiled at her. "I was remembering when Mason was born. Your mother and I were so happy to welcome our first grandchild." He paused. "Wouldn't mind welcoming another, by and by."

"I'd love to accommodate you," she said, trying to keep things light. "But the problem is, I don't have a husband."

"Yet." Again, he looked meaningfully toward the guesthouse. "But there's this real nice guy living next door to you for the summer…"

Was her father matchmaking between her and Emilio? "Don't go there," she said.

"Okay, okay, enough said. I have chores of my own." He strode over toward the auto repair shop.

Kitty smiled as she watched him walking away, stopping to comment on Mason's good work weeding the garden. She was so fond of him. He was her father in every sense that mattered, even though she'd recently learned he wasn't her biological father.

"Don't you close *your* mind to love, either!" she yelled after him.

Dad looked back and waved a hand dismissively, but it seemed to her that his face was a little bit red.

That was interesting. Very interesting. What might be going on in her father's life?

Emilio parked his SUV at the lakefront beach parking lot, and they all piled out—Kitty from the passenger seat, and the three kids from the back. Nora helped Alice out of her car seat with the expertise of long experience.

Emilio had to admit that it was nice to be here with a woman—his dear friend Kitty—and their three kids.

Yes, he was already starting to think of Nora and Alice as his kids.

Around them were multiple family groups, some pulling swimming and picnic supplies out of their vehicles and others already settled on the grassy lawn that led down to the sandy lakefront. He liked the sense of belonging he felt, joining them with a family of his own.

Moreover, he thought it was good for

Alice and Nora to feel like they were part of a family. A family that did healthy things together, not a family that got into fights and then used drugs or alcohol to mask the pain.

As they all walked toward the beach, Emilio noticed the back of Nora's outfit for the first time and his jaw almost dropped.

She wore a black bathing suit, but the striking thing was her cover-up. It was black and had evidently started life as a plain T-shirt. But the entire back of it was cut out and woven back together to make a spiderweb. And was that a plastic spider attached to her shoulder blade?

Maybe this was where he should draw the line. He wasn't afraid of spiders, but that getup looked creepy.

Mason was walking behind Nora, studying her shirt. "Cool spider," he said.

Cool wasn't the word Emilio would have used. But he liked the half smile that lifted Nora's mouth.

Emilio looked at Kitty, trying to get a

clue of how he ought to handle this latest fashion statement.

Kitty had walked closer and was studying the back of Nora's cover-up. "That took a lot of talent," she said. "Did you make it yourself?" And they were off, talking about DIY clothing—whatever that was—and about all the different crafty things you could do with T-shirts.

Emilio didn't like it. Why would a beautiful young girl like Nora cover herself in weird cobweb clothes? But he decided he'd do what Kitty had suggested earlier: He'd choose his battles. Nora had reluctantly helped him clean up the suite and guided Alice in picking up her toys, so they were off to some kind of a start with chores. That was enough for today.

They reached the end of the lawn, where the sandy beach started, and set up their blankets and beach umbrella there. That way, they could be on the grass or down in the sand as they preferred.

As Nora pulled a comic book and water bottle out of her beach bag, a couple of other girls walked by. They looked at Nora's outfit, looked at each other and started giggling.

Emilio forgot everything he knew about leaving kids to fight their own battles. He walked over and stood between Nora and the snotty girls. "Was there something you wanted to say to us?" he asked, giving them a level glare.

"No!"

"No, we were just leaving."

The two girls hurried away, and Emilio turned back to see that both Nora and Kitty were looking at him.

"What?" he asked.

The two of them looked at each other and gave simultaneous eye rolls.

"Hey, Nora. Hey, Ms. MacIntyre." The boy Emilio had seen getting way too close to Nora in the library approached them. Beside him was a girl who had to be his twin sister.

"Hey, guys," Nora said, sounding more upbeat than usual.

Emilio tensed. He wanted Nora to make

friends—obviously that was important at her age. But he was skeptical about this boy's motives.

"Want to come hang out with us?" the girl asked.

Nora smiled but then glanced over at Alice. "I have to bring my sister. Is that okay?"

Emilio frowned. He felt the event going out of his control. On the other hand, Alice would play a kind of chaperone role.

Kitty elbowed him gently, as if to say, *Watch me.*

She walked over and greeted the twins. Then she looked at Nora. "You know, Alice is pretty happy digging in the sand. She can stay with us if you want to hang out with the twins. They could show you around the area."

Nora looked torn. She walked over and squatted down by Alice. "Are you okay if I go walk around with my friends for a little bit?"

Alice looked up, seemed to check that

Emilio was there, and nodded. "I okay," she said.

"Great!" Nora picked up her bag, and the three preteens started to walk away.

"Wait a minute." Emilio cleared his throat. "You stay close by," he said to Nora.

"Stay where you can see us," Kitty added, directing her comment to Izzy and Ishmael.

"We will." The three of them walked off, talking. Mason was down at the edge of the water, splashing with another couple of kids.

Alice dug in the sand, singing to herself.

Kitty spread out a blanket and pulled a book and a soda out of her beach bag. She glanced over at him. "You feel okay about how that went, with Nora?"

"I guess," he said, looking over to where he could still see the three preteens talking. "I would rather she stayed nearby all the time, but she's too old for that, isn't she?"

"Yeah, she needs some independence. But it's fair to say for her to stay where she can see you. You don't know how things will go. And she's new to the area. She doesn't know her way around yet."

"I don't know if I'll ever figure this out," Emilio said. "You're really good with kids, though."

"You will be, too, because you care," she said. Then she looked down at the water. "Are you gonna swim? Should we race to the dock?"

Emilio grinned. There was a floating dock out in the middle of the lake, and he couldn't count the number of times he and Kitty had raced each other. They were both strong swimmers, evenly matched.

"We better not," he said. "We have to keep an eye on the kids. But I'll wade with you if you want. We could take Alice in."

"Sounds good. It's hot out." She pulled off her T-shirt and shorts, looking away in a way that told him she was a little self-conscious.

She had no reason to be. She looked beautiful in her modest swimsuit—really more of a swim dress, made like something an old movie star would wear. It was red with white polka dots, and she looked really, really pretty in it.

There were a lot of women around who wore much more revealing swimsuits, but Emilio liked that Kitty was a little more covered up. She wasn't trying too hard or showing off.

He kicked off his old canvas beach shoes and took a couple of steps toward the water. "Ready?"

She raised an eyebrow. "You're wearing a T-shirt? You never used to."

"Yeah. I have some scars. Not supposed to get too much sun on them."

"You have… Oh." She softened.

She'd probably lose that admiring look if she saw the long stripe across his chest and the crisscrosses on his back. They weren't pretty. But he couldn't complain. He'd gotten off better than a lot of guys.

He knelt beside Alice. "Want to go in the lake, sugar pie?"

She looked toward the water and then up at him. "I scared."

"I'll hold on to you, and we'll only go as far as you want to, okay?"

"Okay," she said and held out her arms to him.

Tenderness squeezed his heart. Poor little Alice—she probably hadn't been to a lake before. She didn't even have a proper swimsuit, just a pair of shorts and a shirt.

As he walked into the water, holding Alice carefully, dipping her toes in and loving the sound of her giggles, his commitment grew. He was going to make sure that Alice and Nora had chores and swimming lessons and a family they could count on.

When they got back to the blankets, Emilio was glad to see that the twins were there with Nora. They spread out a blanket nearby, and all of them were laughing at something on Nora's tablet.

Emilio set Alice down, and she toddled over to her sister, hugging her and getting her wet, making Nora squeal. That in turn made Alice laugh. It was nice to see the girls having fun together.

Kitty's phone had been buzzing when they got back, and she was talking on it now, looking increasingly upset.

She ended the call and shook her head. "We're in trouble."

"Why, what's wrong?"

"It's the fireworks company that I hired to do the display for the Fourth of July. They've gone bankrupt, so they can't fulfill their contract."

Relief washed over Emilio. Maybe he could avoid being around fireworks—avoid having a bad reaction. "That's great news," he said before he could stop himself.

"What? It's a disaster!" She frowned. "It's going to be hard to get another company to do them at this late date. Everyone will be booked."

"Yeah."

"Maybe we could do some kind of a contest of home fireworks. Now that so much stuff is legal in Pennsylvania, people do some pretty good displays."

Emilio winced, thinking of the sporadic nature of home fireworks. "That could be even worse," he said.

"Worse? What do you mean? Worse than what?" She studied him curiously.

He sighed. "There's something I didn't tell you about me and the Fourth of July."

"What's that?"

"I don't like fireworks. Ever since being overseas."

She stared at him, her expression confused, and then the light dawned. "PTSD? You don't have it, do you?"

He shrugged, nodded. "Yeah. I do. It's not that bad, but fireworks aren't my favorite."

"Oh, wow." Her forehead wrinkled.

He hated the thought of her being put off by his condition or, even worse, pitying him. "Mine's not as bad as some. I know people who hit the ground whenever they hear a car backfiring."

"So yours isn't that bad. But you just… don't care for fireworks."

"Right." He was understating it, but hopefully that would be enough to get the message across. "Fourth of July fireworks aren't the best tradition for vets. I mean, there are plenty who don't mind them at all. But some do. A fair number of us. So fireworks celebrations are a problem."

"And we should be celebrating veterans," she said, her forehead creasing. "After all, we owe you our independence. But…"

He waited. He really wondered where she would come down on the question. Kitty was thoughtful, a compassionate person, but she also seemed desperate to put on an event that everyone would find impressive.

Which probably meant fireworks.

What she said next confirmed his thoughts. "I really think if we don't have fireworks, people will be upset. Actually, I'll be upset, too. I love fireworks."

He nodded. "I used to. Not anymore."

"So…when were you planning to tell me you couldn't deal with the main part of a Fourth of July celebration?"

Emilio frowned. "Is it really the main part? What about the flags and the parades and the barbecues?"

"Sure, but it's fireworks people really expect on the Fourth. Everyone's going to be so disappointed if we don't have them."

This discussion wasn't going the way he'd hoped it would. "Including you," he said.

"Including me, and all the kids in town. Emilio, we've got to have them."

He sighed. He'd hoped she would understand and fall in line with his preferences, but after all, she was her own person. She didn't have to agree with him, and she was the one in charge of the celebration. He was basically just a consultant, so if she felt like they had to go for a big old fireworks show, he'd manage. With earplugs and sunglasses and a lot of mental preparation. "It's part of the tradition, I guess."

"I really want it all to go well," she fretted. "You have a point, but I'm worried. And I have to wonder, if you feel this way about Independence Day celebrations, do you really want to help me with this one? Would you rather just kind of escape?"

He sat back, wiping off with a towel. "We don't have to figure it all out today. Let's think on it and pray about it."

"Okay." She reached out and squeezed his hand. "I'm sorry. I don't mean to be insensitive. I'll definitely pray about it."

"Thank you." He looked into her eyes, wide and compassionate and pretty, and then he couldn't seem to look away. The sounds around them faded—the kids' laughter, the lifeguards' shouting, a dog barking. It was as if, in all the world, it was just the two of them.

Dizzy. He felt dizzy. Like he wanted to hold on to her.

Wow. What on earth?

"Can you keep an eye on Alice and Nora for a couple minutes? I'm going back in the water." Without waiting for an answer, he stood. He jogged down to the beach, waded quickly into the lake and swam hard toward the dock. He sliced through the cold water, muscles working, the sound of the other swimmers muted.

The whole time he was thinking in rhythm with his swimming strokes. *No. No. No.*

He couldn't let himself get attracted to his best friend. That would ruin everything.

Chapter Five

Kitty's steps slowed as she walked toward the picnic pavilion beside the church on Sunday. She was carrying a big tray of her famous fried chicken, which she'd gotten up early to make and then had stowed in a thermal container before the church service. It smelled fantastic, and people would be happy she'd brought it. But even so, her mood was dark.

Church usually improved her mood. Not today. She'd tried to pray, tried to focus on worship, but without success.

She knew she should get outside of herself and stop focusing on her own problems. She and Mason were healthy, they had money enough to get by and she was blessed with a supportive family and friends. Despite the issues caused by her ex, she loved her hometown.

And yet…she couldn't stop worrying. She had to figure out what to do about the Fourth of July celebration now that the fireworks company had canceled…and now that she'd learned Emilio didn't really want that kind of celebration anyway.

Emilio. Why had he agreed to help when he didn't like traditional celebrations? When he couldn't handle them, when they threw him into stress and a possible PTSD attack?

Kitty knew she shouldn't be angry at Emilio. He couldn't help having PTSD. Maybe she was mad at herself for not thinking through the ramifications of fireworks; she should have been more sensitive. But either way, she had a problem on her hands. She was in charge of the celebration, and she had to figure out how to salvage it now that the fireworks company had backed out.

Most of the congregation was settling at the three long picnic tables covered with paper tablecloths. A couple of guys were grilling burgers, sending that unmistakable and delicious fragrance over the gathering. At one end of the shelter house, a food table was already laden with potato salad, coleslaw and corn on the cob, along with watermelon and mouthwatering desserts.

The church did after-service luncheons at least once a month, but the summer ones were the best of all.

"Over here, Kitty!" Gemma beckoned from one of the tables. As soon as Kitty arrived, she snagged a piece of chicken. Most of the others in the vicinity followed suit, so that the container was only half-full by the time she took it up to set with the other food.

She scanned the area, looking for Mason. He was running around with a couple other boys, letting loose the pent-up energy left over from an hour of sitting still in church. When she caught his eye, she waved, pointing to the food, and he nodded. He'd be over to fill a plate soon, she knew—Mason was a good eater, and lately, he was always hungry.

She chatted with a few people and made herself a plate. When she returned to Gemma's table, there was Emilio, sitting with a plate in front of him and Alice on his lap.

The only empty space was across from him. Which was fine. They were friends— good friends, old friends.

She set her plate down. "Where's Nora?" she asked Emilio as she sat down. The preteen had reluctantly sat in the section of church they called the teen corral, and Kitty was wondering how it had gone for her.

"She said she'd be out in a minute," Emilio said. "I'm watching for her."

The talk was general as everyone dug into the meal, and Kitty started to feel better. Maybe she'd just been hungry. She caught up with Gemma and laughed to see Alice's delight in the hot dog Emilio cut up for her. Then Juniper, Gemma's daughter, had to have a cut-up hot dog, too, and would only accept one cut up by Emilio.

When Nora came toward the pavilion, walking beside a group of teens and pre-teens, Emilio started to stand.

Kitty kicked him under the table, shaking her head.

He looked at her, a confused expression on his face. "What?"

"Give her a minute," Kitty said quietly. "Maybe she's making friends."

Sure enough, Nora glanced over toward them but then sat with the other young people.

Others at their table had noticed the arrival of the small group of adolescents. "I don't understand the way teenagers dress these days," Mrs. Miller said. "All that black, in the summer, no less!"

"I don't get it, either," Emilio said, "even though one of them is mine." He pointed out Nora.

Alice contributed by saying proudly, "Nora my sister."

"Does that boy beside her have a safety pin in his ear?" somebody else asked.

Kitty saw Emilio studying the group. Nora was sitting beside Ishmael and Izzy. Ishmael probably did have a safety pin in his ear. "Kids that age are exploring ways to express themselves," she said. "I see it in the classroom all the time. It's fascinating."

"Hey, they came to church, and that's what's important." Gemma looked around the table. "Right?"

"Right," a couple of people said firmly.

Mrs. Miller studied Gemma through narrowed eyes. Gemma wore huge hoop earrings, especially visible on the shaved side of her head, and a bright purple dress.

Kitty tried not to giggle. Gemma was her own person, and she definitely expressed her unique personality through her clothing choices. Kitty would defy anyone to tell her she had to conform.

Pastor Kevin came over and everyone

stopped eating to greet him. A widower, he was in his sixties—silver-haired, energetic and fit.

After saying hello to the others, introducing himself to Emilio and handing Alice a small plastic Jonah and the whale toy, the pastor addressed Kitty. "How are plans for the Fourth coming?" he asked.

"Yeah, we're all excited about it," Joe Turner, a big beefy grandfather, said. "It's my favorite holiday." Then he looked abashed as he addressed the pastor. "I mean, Christmas and Easter are more important, but as far as celebrations…you can't beat the Fourth."

"I've always loved fireworks," Mrs. Miller said. "And they've gotten better and better. I can't wait to see what they're like this year."

Emilio and Kitty exchanged glances. *See, everyone loves fireworks*, she telegraphed mentally.

He raised an eyebrow. He knew what she was thinking.

"I was hoping we could get the church

involved in the event," Pastor Kevin said. "Holiday Point, just down the river, had a lot of success with that. It's too late to plan a big church event, but maybe we could have a booth? And some of you folks who love the Fourth could run it."

Pastor Kevin was hard to resist, and several of those at the table agreed to help.

As people finished eating and some seats opened up, Nora came over and sat on the bench beside Emilio. Alice climbed into her lap and leaned against her, sucking her thumb. Nora smiled and murmured to her, running a hand over her hair, combing through it gently with her fingers.

The love between the two sisters was palpable and sweet, and even those who had questioned the way teenagers dressed smiled to see it.

Over dessert, people started reminiscing about the Fourth of July—big celebrations, small ones, how things had changed when fireworks became legal in Pennsylvania.

"I'm excited to see fireworks," Nora said shyly. "We never went to Fourth of July fireworks before, but it sounds cool."

Everyone fell over themselves explaining what fireworks were like, seeming to sympathize with children who'd been so deprived of a common celebration.

Emilio rubbed the back of his neck. He had to be ambivalent now, because Kitty knew for a fact that he was keen on giving his nieces everything they'd missed in their earlier childhood.

All this talk was raising the stakes for the event.

"Oh, Kitty," Mrs. Stiffler, a major town gossip, started. She hadn't been eating with them, but she'd stopped by their table to chat. "Will Mason's father be involved again this year?"

People's forks froze on the way to their mouths. All eyes went to Kitty. Her ex had actually spoken at last year's celebration—a speech full of lies about his own military history—just before the truth about his bad-conduct discharge had come out.

People were nudging each other. Someone made a shushing sound.

"No, he won't be involved," Kitty said firmly.

"Oh, good, I was worried." Mrs. Stiffler looked avid. "Because last year—"

"I'm running the event," Kitty interrupted, "and he won't be involved."

Someone changed the subject. Kitty looked away, trying to cool her hot face, and saw Mason running along with a couple other kids. They were flying a kite. He looked happy and carefree.

The town still remembered what had happened—they remembered her ex's lies. She needed to push last year out of their minds with a fantastic celebration.

But how? She had hoped to figure it out today, but she had no answer as to what to do. And now, after hearing everyone's excitement about the event to come, it mattered even more.

On Sunday night, Emilio was about to text Kitty when he saw her talking with some guests who'd arrived earlier in the day for the week.

Once they left, he approached her. "Can we talk?"

She forked her fingers through her hair and nodded. "Sure, if we can sit over on my porch. I want to be able to hear Mason if he needs anything. Will that work for you?"

"Sure." He'd left Nora in charge of Alice, who was sleeping. She'd promised to come get him if there were any problems.

They settled on Kitty's porch, where rocking chairs and hanging flower baskets made for a cozy environment. But what he had to talk about wasn't cozy.

"Look, I'm sorry about my lack of enthusiasm for fireworks. I could tell from the group's conversation today that it's important." He studied her face. "Do you want me to back out?"

"No, no." Kitty sounded troubled. "I don't want you to back out entirely."

"Are you sure? Maybe you could get

another veteran involved, someone who doesn't have my issues. Or I can help with everything else, the vendors and kids' games and music, but just kind of disappear when the fireworks happen. Maybe the veterans who struggle would even want to do an alternate event, and I could organize that."

Kitty frowned. "That seems wrong, separating those vets who struggle from everyone else."

It seemed wrong to Emilio, too. But he couldn't figure out a compromise. Fireworks involved flashing lights and loud booming sounds, which were a big problem to some veterans, himself included. And yet, almost everyone else wanted fireworks.

"I've planned for some game booths, and I've been talking to a couple of food truck owners about handling the food. But…without fireworks, it'll be just like every other festival."

"Now wait a minute," he said. "We can make the game booths cool. Have you thought about mini handball? Or target golf? The guys at the base loved those. I could arrange it."

"That's…a good idea," she said, sounding reluctant.

"And maybe, instead of food trucks, enlist some guys in the community to do the grilling. That way, people have more to do and feel more involved."

She made a couple of notes. "That could work."

He sighed. "But you don't think that'll satisfy folks."

"Not really. I keep thinking and thinking about it, and I just can't figure out any kind of exciting end to the event that's half as good as fireworks." She tilted her head to one side, looking at him from beneath thick, pretty eyelashes. "Are you gonna hate me if I keep trying to find more fireworks companies?"

"Hate you?" He reached over and squeezed her hand. "I could never hate you. And you made a plan for a celebration with fireworks before I ever got involved." In his heart, he wished she could understand what all the loud noises and flashing lights meant to him. But there was no way a civilian could. Not unless they'd been involved in some violent event involving gunfire or explosions themselves, which, thankfully, Kitty hadn't.

"Then… I guess I'll try to find more fireworks companies. I don't know if I even can, but I'll try. And I'll keep my ears open for other options."

That was reasonable. "I'll talk to the guys at the VFW about it all—see how people feel about fireworks or about having an alternative event. I can also see if they have ideas for games or displays that'll make the whole thing more exciting."

"Thanks for working with me on it," she said. She was rocking gently in her chair. Around them, in the twilight, the sound of crickets rose and fell.

He loved the peace of his hometown,

and despite the problems, he was glad he'd come. "You're welcome. I want to do it."

Their eyes met, and their gazes held. *Again.* Emilio needed to stop that in its tracks, so he stood.

And then the gentleman in him had to hold out his hand to help her get up…and the man in him didn't want to let go. The feel of her delicate hand in his was too appealing.

Grabbing the bull by the horns, he said, "This is weird."

"Yeah." She seemed to know exactly what he meant.

They were standing, facing each other, holding hands.

And she was absolutely beautiful, her hair curling past slender shoulders, her eyes wide, her mouth full and pretty.

He wanted to kiss her more than anything he'd wanted in a really, really long time. He leaned a little forward.

She didn't pull away.

His heart pumped harder.

Next door, the screen door banged, and they jumped apart guiltily.

Nora strode across the lawn between the guesthouse and Kitty's place. "Alice is having dreams, and you said to come and get you," she said. "Sorry to interrupt."

"You're not interrupting," Emilio said firmly. In his head, he added, *You* are *interrupting, but I'm glad you did.*

Because if she hadn't, he would have kissed his best friend and ruined everything.

Emilio followed Nora into the house, filled with a mixture of longing and relief and worry.

Worry predominated. Kitty had known what he wanted to do. And yeah, in the moment she'd seemed willing. But he shouldn't have made even the slightest move toward her, because he couldn't let things go in that direction.

Nora was waiting for him inside their suite. "Thought you two were just friends," she said in a snotty voice.

"We are," he said. He headed into the bedroom where Alice was sleeping. "She seems okay now. What was she doing?"

Nora followed him out of the bedroom. "She was thrashing around and whining. Guess I shouldn't have broken in on you and Kitty." She crossed her arms over her chest, glaring at him. "Looked to me like you two are a little more than friends."

"Well, it may have looked that way, but Kitty and I are just friends. I've made a commitment to that. My priority is you girls."

Nora looked at him skeptically. "Why would you have us for your priority when you could get with a lady like Kitty?"

And there it was, Emilio thought. Nora felt threatened by the possibility of him getting into a relationship and then neglecting her and Alice.

He sat down on the arm of the couch so that he was more at Nora's level and could hold her gaze. "You girls are my family. I've made a commitment to you, and I want to take care of you. Not just for a little while, but until you're grown enough to take care of yourselves."

"We were taking care of ourselves a long time ago," Nora muttered.

"I know you had too much responsibility. I regret that that happened, but it's not going to happen again. I'm your uncle and I'm your guardian. I'm taking care of you."

He glanced at the clock. "And since I'm in charge of you, I think you probably ought to get to bed."

"Humph," Nora said. She made a face at him, but in a half-joking way. "I'm going to bed because I want to, not because you told me to."

He shook his head. "Nora, Nora, Nora. Twelve years old and already acting like you run the world."

"Women *do* run the world. Just ask your *friend* Kitty." She stuck out her tongue at him and then half walked, half swaggered into her bedroom.

Emilio had to smile. Nora was a handful, but he was starting to figure her out. He had done the right thing tonight, reassuring her. It was a success in an arena where he hadn't been having a whole lot of them.

The problem was, Nora had detected something real. Emilio did long to hold Kitty. He did think she was about the best woman he'd ever known, and he was starting to feel romantic toward her.

But romance would kill their friendship. It would upset the balance he was gaining with Nora and Alice.

And it wouldn't last. That was the nature of the beast.

So his longing to hold Kitty, to build some kind of romantic relationship with her, had to be shoved aside. His personal desires didn't matter. He had two girls to take care of, and he needed them to have stability. Needed them to know they had him, that he was focused on them and their needs.

He would chalk up that little interlude with Kitty as a mistake and move on.

And he wouldn't make the same mistake again.

Chapter Six

Kitty spent most of the next day researching fireworks options and trying to forget about that unnerving near-kiss with Emilio last night.

Why had it happened? What had possessed Emilio to look at her that way, lean in, touch her arm?

Why hadn't she herself just backed away? Why hadn't she made a joke and gone inside?

It was probably just the late-night setting. Moonlight, the fragrance of night-blooming jasmine wafting through the air, the sound of the crickets rising and falling. The way Emilio had looked. And the way he'd looked at her.

She had to keep reminding herself: This was Emilio. Her old friend—really, her best friend. And yes, she'd felt some odd vibes with him before, but last night they'd come close to actually doing something about them, acknowledging them, maybe even moving from the friend zone into something more.

Which would be a huge disaster.

It had been hard enough on Mason when she and Jeff had broken up. The move, the loss of friends, the fact that his dad was unpredictable in his visits and phone calls…all of it was hard on him. And although Kitty's father, and her brother, Jake, had picked up the slack and were serving as wonderful male role models, Mason still needed stability, not change.

No way was she going to get into another relationship that could so easily end and cause trauma. She wasn't up for it, and Mason wasn't up for it. She was just getting stabilized here, settled in her hometown with her family around her. She definitely didn't want to rock that boat.

And Emilio didn't, either. He didn't really want to be involved with her except as a friend, she was sure of it. He wanted to focus on his nieces, and rightly so. It had probably just been the moonlight for him, too.

Determinedly, she forced herself to work on finding a replacement fireworks vendor. She made phone calls and scoured the internet, but her research didn't turn up any promising options. Most of the companies in the region were already booked full with Fourth of July shows.

A dull drum of worry thudded in her chest. Would they have to do a weak, no-fun, below-average movie night? That wouldn't be enough to repair the reputation her ex had started for her family last year, with his lies.

"Mom, Mom!" Mason came running into the house. "Uncle Jake's home!"

Kitty looked at the clock and was surprised to see that it was already 4:00 p.m. She pushed aside her laptop and hurried outside, following Mason. She greeted her brother with a huge hug.

Everybody piled into the guesthouse—her brother, Jake, his fiancée, Summer, and her two children, Wyatt and Rylee. Kitty helped carry suitcases and bags and boxes to Summer and her kids' suite and then to Jake's. The two of them would be getting married and moving out into a temporary home down the road while their own place was being built. And none too soon, because the guesthouse was starting to attract more guests and the suites they had occupied would be needed. Summer could continue to manage the guesthouse's day-to-day operations, conveniently living right down the street.

After most of the stuff was put away, they all gathered in the kitchen. Kitty studied Jake with satisfaction. He looked well rested and so, so happy. She was thrilled that he and Summer had found each other.

Dad was looking happy, too, as he puttered around setting out cheese and crackers to hold everyone over until dinner. He was close to Jake, of course, always had been. Not every father and son could run a business together and get along, but Dad and Jake enjoyed working together in the auto repair shop next door.

Dad had come to love Summer and her kids as well. They all had.

There was a tap on the wall beside the door. "Okay if we come in to say hello?" Emilio asked, leaning into the kitchen with Alice and Nora behind him.

"Come in, come in," Kitty and her father said, practically in unison.

The girls stopped at the door, and Nora put a hand on Alice's shoulder.

"Well, look what the cat dragged in," Jake said, shaking Emilio's hand vigorously. "And who are these two pretty girls?"

Jake and Emilio had known each other growing up, though Jake was nine years older. Kitty had told Jake that Emilio was bringing his nieces to stay for the summer, but love had made her brother a little distracted.

Emilio introduced the girls, and then Jake introduced Summer and her kids. Mason was already talking to Wyatt about all the things they'd do this summer. The two boys were almost the same age and had become fast friends when Summer's family had moved here just a few months ago.

Alice looked a little frightened of all the activity, and Dad went over, knelt beside her and put an arm around her.

He was explaining who everyone was when four-year-old Rylee marched over to the pair and faced them, putting her hands on her hips. "That's *my* Mr. Grandpa," she said.

Everybody laughed except Alice, who looked up at Nora. "We have grandpa?" she asked.

"No. We have Uncle Emilio. That's all."

The room went quiet.

Kitty shot a glance at Emilio. His face was stricken. The rest of the adults looked stricken, too. Alice and Nora were alone in the world except for Emilio.

No wonder they were scared he'd be taken away from them.

Mason went over to Alice and knelt in front of her. "He's really my grandpa," he said, pointing at Kitty's father. "But you can share him, just like Rylee does."

Dad tried to say something, cleared his throat and ended up giving Mason, Rylee and Alice a giant hug instead. Then he got to his feet and hugged Nora and Wyatt, both of whom squirmed a little but looked pleased nonetheless.

Warmth filled Kitty's heart as she went to put an arm around her father. He wasn't her biological father, either, but although he'd suspected that fact, he'd raised her as his own with no complaint. He wasn't a showy man, but he had a heart as big as the state of Pennsylvania. Now, he was sharing it with children who needed a wise, loving grandfather figure. "You're the best, Dad," she said, hugging him fiercely.

They ordered pizza for dinner, and Jake and Summer insisted that Emilio and the girls join them. A couple of the guesthouse visitors stopped by and were invited in, too. That made Kitty smile.

She'd grown up with hospitality at the heart of her life. The guesthouse had been her home, but she'd grown used to sharing it with visitors on a regular basis. That had been her parents' ethos, and she was glad that her father was continuing the tradition.

After dinner, everyone went their separate ways. Nora went out to the swing by the river with a graphic novel. Rylee had gotten over her upset with Alice and realized, apparently, that this was someone new to play with and boss around. The two girls were chasing Rylee's kittens around the guesthouse, with Rylee shouting instructions to Alice on the best way to catch and interact with them.

Summer, Kitty and Emilio sat in rockers on the guesthouse's front porch. "You know," Summer said to Emilio, "we could exchange some babysitting for the summer. Gemma—you know, Gemma, next door? Anyway, she has a little girl, Juniper, who's the same age as Rylee. We babysit for each other all the time. Alice would be welcome to join in."

"That's a great idea," Kitty said. "You have to pay attention and grab this kind of opportunity," she explained to Emilio. "This is the mom grapevine—or really, the parent grapevine."

"I'm down with that," Emilio said. "It would be really good for Alice to be with some girls closer to her own age. I'm glad to do my share of supervising, if you'll let me. Just be aware, I'm pretty new to all this."

"Of course," Summer said kindly. "Alice seems like a sweet little girl."

"She is." Emilio looked toward the

swing where Nora sat, staring out at the river. "Now, I just have to figure out some activities for that one."

"Something will work out," Kitty assured him.

Jake came by then and talked Emilio into coming down to the river for a little fishing. After they walked away, Summer turned to Kitty and grabbed her arm. "Are the two of you dating?"

"No! No way." Even as she said it, Kitty felt her face getting hot. She couldn't be around Emilio without being conscious of him, especially after they'd come so close to kissing the other night.

"Why not?" Summer asked. "He seems like a nice guy, and he's almost as good-looking as Jake. And there's a little bit of a vibe between you."

"No, there's not," Kitty said, even though there was. "Look, I'm no good with relationships. It probably runs in the family." Summer's presence, though welcome, reminded her of their mother's mistakes. Mom had gotten into a long-ago affair with

Summer's father, which they'd only recently discovered, and Kitty was the product of their union. Her mother had patched things up with Dad—the man Kitty considered her real father—and they'd had a long and seemingly happy marriage.

Summer and Kitty were half sisters and glad to have discovered each other. But the situation didn't exactly give Kitty a good impression of marriage.

"You and Emilio sure seem to be bonding as single parents," Summer persisted.

"That's our agreement. I'm helping him learn to be a dad, and he's helping me with the Fourth of July celebration. We're friends—old friends—but nothing more."

"Okay, sure." Summer looked skeptical.

Kitty felt skeptical herself, despite her determination to avoid romance.

A couple of guests came out then, and Summer went over to meet them. She was back in charge of the guesthouse, leaving Kitty in a more supporting role for now.

The guests and Summer came over to the

porch. Mason and Wyatt had come over, too, and were drinking from the hose.

"Hey, Kitty, Mr. and Mrs. Vickers were wondering if there's a good Fourth of July event here in town," Summer said. "They're thinking about coming back for the Fourth."

Kitty's stomach twisted. "Uh, yeah, there's always a big shindig in the park," she said. "Nothing like big-city displays, but it's small-town fun."

Mason had heard the last bit. "Mom's in charge of it, and we're gonna have awesome fireworks!"

"At least, I hope so," Kitty said under her breath.

Emilio and Jake had come back to join them, and after the guests and kids had run off, the four of them stood talking.

"I got the feeling you weren't too sure about the Fourth of July event," Summer said.

"I'm not," Kitty admitted. "The fireworks company I scheduled with just went belly-up, and I'm scrambling to find new people to do the display. Know anyone?"

"I don't, but I'll ask around," Summer said.

Jake frowned at Kitty. "I told you this was gonna be a lot for you. Are you sure you're up to handling it?"

"I have no choice," Kitty said. "I committed to it and I'm doing it."

"And I'm helping out," Emilio said, his voice firm. "That's why Kitty let me come for the summer—on condition that I would help with the Fourth of July event she's organizing. And I will." He looked at her steadily, and she felt warm and supported, as well as a little embarrassed, because Jake and Summer were looking between her and Emilio with interest.

Kitty realized that her goals for the day had not been achieved. Not only had she not found another Fourth of July fireworks company, but she'd also failed to get Emilio off her mind. In fact, he was more there than ever.

* * *

On Tuesday, Emilio found himself longing for the discipline and structure of his military life. Being a parent was so much more confusing and ambiguous.

Like today. It was raining, so he'd worried because Alice and Nora couldn't be outside. Then, Gemma had invited Alice and Rylee over to play with Juniper, so that took care of Alice. But it left Nora at loose ends.

Emilio didn't know what to do with her, but he knew she shouldn't just watch TV or play on her tablet all day.

And then he lit on it: chores. No time like the present to teach Nora how to do laundry. All of them were running low on clothes, and with Nora's fashion consciousness, weird as it was, she would want to have her choice of clean outfits.

They had just carried her and Alice's laundry baskets down to the guesthouse's laundry room and started their first load when there was a knock on the front door. Summer answered, and then she stuck her head into the laundry room. "Company for you, Nora," she said.

Nora brightened, then hurried toward the front door. Emilio followed.

Just as he suspected, it was the twins. "She wants to go to the library," Ishmael said, nodding toward his sister. "Do you want to go along and hang out with us?"

Nora looked so happy that Emilio was tempted to just let her go. That would be the easy route, but he was committed to doing the right thing, not the easy one. "She can't go," he said. "She has chores to do."

"Uncle Emilio!" Nora stared at him, her face a mask of betrayal. "I'll do them later!"

"You'll do them now," he said.

The twins winced, identical in gesture if not in looks. "Later, Nora," the boy said in a sympathetic tone, and they took their leave.

Nora faced him down in the guesthouse parlor, hands on hips. She looked so much like her mother that Emilio felt his throat tighten. He remembered when he and Bianca would get into fights, back in simpler days when their conflicts had to do with the rules of a board game or invasion of one another's space.

But his sister was way beyond that now. Essentially, she was lost to him as well as to her daughters.

Nora glared at him. "I have no friends here except them, and they asked me!"

"I don't want you getting too involved with that boy," Emilio said, keeping his voice low and calm.

"What do you have against him?" Nora's voice rose on every word until she was practically screaming.

The fact that he's a boy, Emilio thought. "I don't know anything about his family, and I don't want to let you just walk off with people I don't know," he said.

"So in other words, I'm stuck here as your servant!" Nora ran into their suite and slammed the door.

"Problems?" came a voice from the doorway. It was Kitty, leaning against the door of the room. "What happened?" she asked him.

He explained that he'd decided to teach Nora how to do laundry, and then the twins had come with their much more appealing invitation.

Kitty tilted her head to one side. "Why didn't you let her go? To the library, of all places?"

"Number one, because I don't want her walking off into town by herself. That's not safe."

"This is a small town." She perched on the arm of a chair. "Don't you remember running all around as a child? Even when we were younger than Nora?"

"Times are different," he said stubbornly.

"Maybe you haven't noticed, but we're stuck in the past around here. In a good way. Our crime rate is pretty close to zero. Plus, she wouldn't be alone. She'd be with two other kids."

Emilio blew out a breath. He was already regretting the fight with Nora, and

Kitty's words didn't help. "I don't want her getting involved with kids I don't know." Even as he said it, he was aware, inside, that he was being unreasonable.

"Their parents seemed nice when I met them on parent night," Kitty said mildly.

Emilio lifted his hands, palms up. "Truth is," he said, "I don't want her getting involved with boys."

"Just think if my parents had felt the same. You and I got to be friends practically when we were babies."

"That's just it." Emilio sank down into one of the wing chairs in the guesthouse's parlor. "Nora is too old for simple friendship and too young for dating."

"You can't make that call for her," Kitty said, perching on the chair opposite him. "Times are different now. Boys and girls hang out together a lot. And besides, it's not just Ishmael—it's Izzy, too. She's a good kid."

"Nora's situation is complicated," Emilio said. "Do you know what she came from?

I can't even imagine the things she's seen in my sister's home. Don't want to."

Kitty's expression grew sympathetic. "I'm sorry about that, Emilio, but that's all the more reason why it's important that she sees normal relationships between men and women—not overly physical ones or casual, transient ones."

"Like ours?" he asked. He felt pushed into the words, pushed by exasperation. Now that he'd said them, he met her eyes steadily.

They hadn't really talked about what had happened the other night, when their relationship had threatened to go beyond platonic. He wondered if she'd thought about it again, like he had.

"Yes, like ours," she said firmly. "Two adults who just happen to be of the opposite sex and who are just friends."

Why did that rub him the wrong way?

Behind him, he could hear Nora stomping around in their suite.

"So…you're just going to keep her sequestered here at the guesthouse for the summer?" Kitty asked.

Emilio leaned back in the chair and stared up at the ceiling. "I don't know. I just know I made her mad, when I really want to build a connection with her."

"Maybe if you could meet the twins' parents, you'd be more comfortable. You could invite them to get pizza or something."

"Maybe," he said doubtfully. Was that the kind of thing he was going to have to do from now on? Socialize with strangers?

But the twins' parents weren't true strangers, he realized. They all had kids of the same age. That meant they should work together rather than at cross-purposes.

If it was what Nora needed, he would do it, however uncomfortable. Again, he found himself longing for the structure and predictability of his military days.

He reached for another topic. "Meanwhile, we have to work on our plans. Any progress finding another company to do fireworks?"

"No. You?"

"No." And he'd actually tried, even though he hated fireworks, but with no success. "Maybe we can meet after the kids are in bed and work on other aspects of the celebration. I spoke more with the pastor about having an information booth for the church. And someone at the VFW suggested adding a dunk tank..." He trailed off, because Kitty was shaking her head slowly.

"Those are good ideas," she said, "but let's work on them tomorrow. I'm not sure late nights together are a good idea."

He met her eyes. She was studying him earnestly, but then she looked away.

He hated the idea of putting restrictions and barriers on their friendship. But given what had happened the other night, how he'd felt, it might be necessary.

"You're probably right," he said. "Tomorrow afternoon, my girls will both be at library programs. For some reason, there's a big afternoon activity for all ages."

"Mason, too," she said. "It's the summer reading kickoff. They make a sort of festival of it, on the front lawn of the library. We can talk in the park area across the way from it. That way, if Alice needs you, you'll be right there."

"Sounds good." Meeting in the park right out in public with a loud kids' activity nearby should keep things platonic. Which was the best idea. He *knew* it was the best idea. The only way to proceed, really.

Kitty needed his help with rescuing the Fourth of July event, and he needed Kitty's help with the girls. But they couldn't let their more-than-friends feelings run away with them. That would ruin everything.

Chapter Seven

By the next day, Emilio had come around to Kitty's point of view. It was a good idea for him and Kitty to meet in the park. The sun was shining and the slight breeze kept things cool. He and Kitty strolled along with Mason and Alice meandering at toddler pace ahead of them. Nora tagged behind, in a grouchy mood.

Emilio had the feeling that Nora wouldn't even have gone to this event if he didn't come along and make her. For some unknown, twelve-year-old girl reason, she was in a rotten mood.

Occasionally in the past, Emilio had

noticed teens acting surly, and he'd wondered why the parents didn't put a stop to the behavior. Now he understood. He'd never judge again.

When they got to the event, just a few minutes before it started, Alice clung to him and didn't want to go with the other children. "I stay with you!" she insisted, clinging to Emilio's leg.

Emilio had a hard time saying no to Alice. She was just so cute and cuddly. But he could tell from Kitty's expression that she didn't think he should just cave and let Alice sit with them. He agreed. Besides, they had work to do.

So he swung Alice into his arms and carried her toward Gemma, who was in the middle of a swarm of kids and adults, smiling and laughing and giving orders. In addition to being their neighbor, apparently she was the librarian in charge of the children's programs.

Despite being the boss of the event, she greeted Emilio and Alice in a friendly way.

"Alice is feeling a little hesitant to join in," he said.

"Oh, we're going to have such a good time!" Gemma was bubbly as usual. She chatted up Alice, telling her about the stories and prizes and balloon animals that would be a part of today's event. In another minute, Alice was clinging to Gemma instead of Emilio.

"Do you want me to try to get her to sit with the other kids?" Emilio asked Gemma. "I hate to have her bothering you."

"Oh, Alice is no bother." Gemma bounced her on one hip. "My Juniper is four and already getting independent. I miss this sweet age."

"I miss Mommy." Alice laid her head against Gemma's shoulder.

Gemma's eyes met Emilio's and she cuddled Alice a little closer.

As Emilio walked away, Alice's words echoed in his head. Of course she missed her mother. Bianca was barely making contact with him or the girls. He had tried last night to get in touch with her, to set up a phone call with Alice and Nora, to no avail. She seemed to trust that Emilio would just care for the girls, and she wasn't even trying to maintain her role.

It was sad and frustrating and infuriating. Emilio missed his sister, the way she used to be, the days when they'd been close. He also felt frustrated that she wasn't even taking the basic step of staying in touch, in case there was some information he needed from her related to the girls' care.

Mostly, he felt furious about the way she was hurting the girls by being absent and unavailable. He'd heard them talking about it, had sat listening to Alice cry for her mother. He'd comforted her, and Nora had, and yet they couldn't replace Bianca. Just look at how Alice had clung to Gemma, a woman she barely knew. She was hungry for mothering Emilio couldn't provide.

Sometimes Emilio hated his sister for abandoning her children this way. Abandoning them for the sake of a new man. For love.

It just went to show that romantic love wasn't the wonderful thing movies made it out to be. It was more of a liability, causing families to fall apart.

He pushed his thoughts aside at the sight of Nora. She was sitting on a stone wall, a little apart from the main group of young readers. That was understandable, since there weren't a whole lot of older kids there.

It was her face that bothered him, though. She looked miserable.

He was walking toward her with the idea of trying to get her to join in the activities when he saw Kitty waving to him. So he changed course and went over to Kitty, who sat on the library steps.

"Do you want to set up on the bench across the street, or stick closer by the kids?"

"I think we should stick closer by. I'm not sure either girl is going to do very well with this. I wish they were just enjoying it like Mason is."

Mason was kneeling with a group of boys, looking at the prizes that would be offered for summer reading. He seemed perfectly content. Would Nora and Alice ever get there?

They were starting to set up on the library steps when Emilio noticed a trio of girls walking by. They were about Nora's age, maybe a little older based on how they were dressed.

Good. Maybe they'd take part in the event and Nora wouldn't feel so alone as one of the older kids.

One of them nudged the others, and they all looked at Nora and laughed.

"Miss Goth does kids' stuff," one of them said, clear as a bell, and they all laughed.

Nora turned away and came toward Emilio, but just then Ishmael showed up and intercepted her. The trio of girls stopped, too.

"I don't even like reading," Nora groused

loudly to Ishmael. "I don't want to be doing this."

"I don't like it, either," Ishmael said.

"But you get straight A's!" one of the girls said.

"And you're a star athlete," said another, looking at Ishmael with admiration.

Nora was looking at Ishmael, a confused, almost betrayed expression on her face.

"She came close to failing English last year," Emilio said to Kitty in a low voice. "I think it had a lot to do with her home situation, because she missed some important parts of her classes."

Nora marched over to Kitty and Emilio. "I don't like reading. I don't wanna do this thing. It's for babies."

"You know," Kitty said, "I'm a middle school English teacher. If you would want to do some catching up over the summer, I'm open to tutoring."

"I don't need tutoring!"

"Yes, you do." Emilio frowned at his niece, partly because she was turning down needed help, and partly because she was being rude.

He didn't expect her to rush away into the library, crying, but that was what she did.

Izzy, Ishmael's twin, came over to them. "Is Nora okay? Want me to check on her?"

"That would be so nice, Izzy," Kitty said. "I think she could use a little girl talk right about now."

"Sure thing," Izzy said, and headed toward the library door that Nora had just gone through.

"Should I have gone after her?" Emilio asked. "I didn't expect her to start crying. I was just giving her some feedback."

"Actually," Kitty said, "you were giving her orders."

"Well, yeah," he said. "Isn't that my job as her guardian?"

"It might be more important for you to connect with her at this point," Kitty said.

"But I want her to have tutoring. That was such a nice offer on your part, and she totally turned it down."

"I wasn't offended. I'm used to twelve-year-olds." She looked at him earnestly. "Would you like a little feedback?"

"Sure, bring it," he said. Kitty was so cute, trying not to be the bossy teacher she was.

"You need to tell Nora that you needed tutoring when you were in school. Don't hold yourself up above her as this big, perfect authority figure. That's just going to make her feel worse about herself."

"You think I should tell her I did poorly in school?" Emilio had never even considered doing that. He wanted to set a good example, not advertise his failures.

"I think you should model being open to getting help. That's what she needs. And that will help her see that you're real and that you're not judging her."

They went on with plans for the celebration. Kitty had good ideas for decorating the town park with balloons and banners and flags. There would be booths for playing games, and Emilio was glad Kitty was incorporating ones the men would especially enjoy, where they could show off their athletic skills.

As they went on brainstorming ideas and making phone calls, Emilio kept thinking about what Kitty had said: that he should reveal his mistakes and vulnerability to his nieces. He was much more accustomed to the military way of doing things. Some people gave orders, and some people obeyed them, and everybody respected each other.

But Kitty had a point. Being a guardian to his nieces was different. Especially given their ages and backgrounds, they had different needs than an eighteen-year-old recruit.

So he would talk to Nora and try to make up for giving her orders. He would gently encourage her to do tutoring and to participate in the summer reading program.

He supposed it was better that he and Kitty had met in public, that they'd stayed here near the kids, since everybody seemed to be in need of a little extra support today.

But he couldn't help wishing for a little alone time with Kitty. Not just so that they could get things done, but so that he could enjoy her company without having all the worries of his nieces front and center.

On Friday afternoon, Kitty pulled into a rutted driveway in the mountains outside River Haven. Emilio was at her side.

Earlier in the week, they'd started looking at private individuals who might possibly do a firework show, and by using the contacts of everyone they knew, they had found a couple of prospects. This morning, they were meeting with one of them to see whether he might be able to save their celebration.

They approached an A-frame mountain home, slightly run-down but respectable-looking, with a big front porch.

"How do you know this guy?" Emilio asked.

"He's Jake's friend's brother-in-law's cousin," she said, with a wry expression. The truth was, she didn't have much of a connection to this guy, but she was desperate. The Fourth was just three weeks away, and there just didn't seem to be many options for a firework display.

When they stopped and got out of the car, the door of the A-frame opened, and a man came out to greet them. He did look like a mountain man, with a heavy beard and a flannel shirt with the sleeves ripped off. But he was carrying a laptop, and when he approached them, he shook both of their hands with vigor.

That was promising.

"So you're looking for a show?" he asked, gesturing for them to come up on the deck.

Kitty explained their situation. "We're looking for a private individual who might have experience with this sort of thing," she finished up. "From what I've researched, though, I'm not sure we'll be able to make it work legally."

Frank waved a hand. "There are rules, but I can get around them," he said.

"Oh, no, I don't want you to break any—"

"I'm related to the owner of a fireworks franchise," he interrupted. "He would come along and sign the paperwork, so we'd be on his insurance. The selling period in Pennsylvania is June 15 to July 8. We're almost there, so it's a good time to set something up."

Kitty looked at Emilio and shrugged. The man seemed knowledgeable enough.

"Sit down," he said, gesturing to the chairs around a metal table. "I'll show you."

He set up the laptop, pushed a few buttons and showed them a fairly impressive video of a firework show.

Kitty smiled. This might just work out after all. Relief relaxed her shoulders, and she glanced over at Emilio.

He was looking away. Was he unimpressed, or did he have a reaction even to a video of fireworks?

Well, but he had agreed to this, she reassured herself. "It looks like quite a show," she said. "What would that kind of thing cost?"

"We'll work it out," Frank said. "It will be a little more because I need to involve my cousin, but I'd like to help you out. Maybe you'll give me a good recommendation, because I want to get into doing this professionally."

"It does sound promising," she said.

"Are you ready to sign something today?"

Emilio spoke up for the first time. "We have a few people we need to consult before finalizing this," he said.

"Come look at my stash," Frank said. "I can do a preliminary show for you now, in person."

"No, that's okay," Emilio and Kitty said, practically at the same time.

"No, come on, you've got to see this." His voice was even more animated. It was clear he loved what he did.

Frank trotted down the stairs and headed around to the back of the house, and Kitty looked at Emilio and shrugged. "It would be rude not to at least look, wouldn't it?"

"I guess." He shrugged. "Yeah, we can go."

They followed in the direction Frank had gone. At the side of the house was a shed the size of a small garage.

But when Frank flung open the door, it was fitted up basically as an arsenal for fireworks. Just at a glance, Kitty spotted ground spinners and fountains, as well as what looked like bottle rockets, all neatly arranged in racks on the walls.

"Hey, Johnson!" A loud voice rang out from next door, and then a woman, also looking very country in a flannel shirt and cutoff shorts, came over to the fence between the two properties. "Don't you scare my dog with your fireworks!" she yelled.

"Can it!" Frank waved a dismissive hand in the woman's direction.

"I hope you blow the rest of your fingers off!" she yelled. Then she went inside and slammed the door of her house.

"The rest of your fingers?" Kitty asked.

Frank held up his right hand, and for the first time, Kitty realized that his index and middle fingers were missing. "Rookie mistake," he said. "I'm a lot more careful now."

He started describing each different type of firework, moving from section to section on the walls.

"Is this even legal?" Kitty asked uneasily.

"Oh, yeah. Ever since I got cited, I only do legal fireworks."

Kitty was getting a bad feeling. She didn't quite trust this guy to put on a safe, professional show. She glanced at Emilio.

He gave a small head shake.

"So what do you say?" Frank asked. "If we can come to an agreement today, I'll knock the deposit down by twenty percent."

Emilio cleared his throat. "Actually, I think we're likely to go in a different direction."

Relief overcame Kitty. She found it hard

to say no to persistent men, so she was glad Emilio had taken on that task.

"Let me show you just a few things I can do," Frank said. He started pulling fireworks off the wall and carrying them outside.

"No, thanks," Emilio said. "We're going to go a different direction."

At that clear rejection, Frank cursed.

"Hey, there's a lady present," Emilio said mildly.

"Oooh, there's a *lady* present," Frank said in a mocking voice.

"Thanks for taking the time," Kitty said, and they hurried toward the car.

They had almost reached it when there was a sharp, whistling *whoosh* and then an explosion.

A moment later, Kitty hit the ground with a thump. Emilio landed right on top of her.

Chapter Eight

In the absence of more enemy fire, Emilio pulled himself up to a crouch and quickly checked his own arms and legs for injuries. Every sense alert, every nerve tingling, he moved to inspect his fellow soldier. Had he gotten her down in time?

Only it wasn't a fellow soldier. It was Kitty.

Confusion made his chest tight, and sweat rolled down his back. His mind raced, trying to make what he was feeling match what he was seeing.

Green grass, not bare sand. Birds singing, not a cacophony of Middle Eastern dialects.

Kitty.

Not an injured comrade, but Kitty.

His heart rate was still high, his adrenaline flowing. He pulled her to her feet and looked behind them.

Frank was doubled over, laughing.

As he emerged from the nightmare his brain had concocted, Emilio brushed dirt and grass from Kitty's hair with shaking hands. "I'm sorry," he said. "Oh, man, I'm sorry."

"I know who I want to be with in a war zone," she said. She was trying to joke, but she was breathing hard, rubbing her arm, studying his face. "Are you okay?"

He ignored the question. "You're hurt. Let me see." He reached for her arm.

"No, no, I'm fine. Just a few scratches." She stepped backward, and that let him know he'd scared her.

Of course he'd scared her. He'd tackled her like she was a running back on the opposing team. He'd done it to protect her, but it had had the opposite effect. He'd hurt her. Shame washed over him. "I'm really sorry. You're sure you're okay? Nothing's broken?"

"Relax. I'm fine." She smiled at him, lifting her arms and shaking them, spinning around. "See?"

"I see." Reassured, Emilio turned back toward Frank, intending to give the jerk a piece of his mind.

Only now the man was running back toward his house, the neighbor they'd seen before chasing him with a baseball bat. She kept screaming, "You scared Buddy and Duke!" The dogs in question—at least, Emilio figured Buddy and Duke were her dogs—ran alongside her, barking.

This was getting ridiculous. Emilio looked back at Kitty. She was giggling, but the sound was slightly hysterical. She grabbed his hand. "Come on, let's get out while we can." She led him toward the passenger side of her car and opened it, and he got in.

Now his legs felt like they could barely support him, and his hands were shaking.

Aftereffects.

When they reached the main road, she pulled over and looked at him. "So…your PTSD is pretty serious."

"It can be. If I know to expect a trigger, I handle it much better. That was a surprise."

"Yeah, it was. What a jerk."

"I really am sorry I knocked you down. You'll have bruises at a minimum."

"It's okay," she said. She reached over and touched his hand briefly. "That's what it took to knock sense into me. It's not fair to do that to vets who fought for our independence."

"Fair or not, it's a reality. Even if the town didn't do a display, plenty of individuals would. I don't want to spoil the fun. Fireworks are cool, and the girls are looking forward to it. Everyone in town is looking forward to it."

She shook her head decisively. "No. We're not doing fireworks." She pulled out onto the highway and headed toward River Haven.

Emilio looked out at the pine trees, into the woods, dappled with sunlight, that they were driving past.

He didn't know what to think. He truly didn't want to be a spoilsport. But he also didn't want to cause himself, or his fellow vets, the kind of trauma that he just experienced, or worse.

"Let's keep thinking about what to do in place of fireworks," she said.

He had to marvel at how calmly she was taking the whole incident. "Thank you," he said.

"For what? Nearly giving you a heart attack? After all, it was my idea to try to work with dear old Frank."

"No. For caring, and for not being mad that I knocked you down."

"Of course." She patted his arm and kept driving.

Emilio leaned against his headrest, letting his tense muscles relax. He felt a killer headache coming on and hoped he could calm it with over-the-counter meds.

He'd love to have a quiet night to recover

at home, but that wasn't to be. There was a cookout tonight at the home of Nora's new friends, the twins, and as a good guardian, he had to attend.

As Kitty got ready for the cookout that evening, she felt shaken.

Not just because Emilio had knocked her to the ground, jolting her bones and giving her a smattering of bruises. But because of what it meant.

For one thing, it meant that Emilio was a very protective man, and she couldn't deny she found that attractive. He'd tried to protect her with his body. If they'd been in real danger, he would've saved her, even if it meant putting himself in harm's way. The thought of that made her heart pound a little faster.

So did the memory of his protective arms around her, shielding her.

Yet the very fact that his heroism appealed to her so much was a concern. She was bad at relationships. She didn't do them, not anymore. She knew herself. She didn't make good decisions about men. She shouldn't trust her instincts and feelings.

And thus, this warm, emotional feeling toward Emilio was not something to be happy about. It was a big red flag saying, *stop, don't go there.*

So she wouldn't.

She forced herself to stop thinking about Emilio's protectiveness and to start thinking about what his reaction meant for the Fourth of July celebration.

He'd told her before that he didn't like fireworks. Okay, that had been a bummer. She'd felt bad for him. But it hadn't changed her determination to have a fireworks show.

Now, she understood viscerally what it meant when he said he didn't like fireworks. It meant that they took him straight back to the battlefield. It meant that he had a major stress reaction that left him shaking and drained.

No way did she want to be responsible for causing that reaction in a man she cared about. And in the many other veterans who felt the same way.

To hurt those who had fought for their independence by causing them pain now… that wasn't the kind of person she wanted to be.

Then what are you going to do instead?

If she put on a quiet, boring event, people would talk. They would talk about her and her lack of planning ability, and they would talk about her ex, who had shown his own lack of patriotism by lying at last year's event.

And all that would come down on Mason. In a small town, it was hard to escape being identified with your family. People figured that if your parents were a certain way, you were that way as well.

So she was in a spot. She couldn't have fireworks, but she couldn't *not* have fireworks.

In the mirror, she checked herself from different angles. Maybe she should wear a dressier shirt, not this faded red "Readers Are Leaders" one. And was there time to straighten her hair?

She ran her fingers through it and then turned away from the mirror, annoyed with herself. She was primping and worrying about her looks because Emilio would be at the cookout, and that was ridiculous. He'd seen her in all kinds of dirty, messy clothes as a kid, and there was no reason to change that now.

Instead, she needed to let this dilemma simmer in her mind. To remember her own sage advice to her students, when they struggled with what to do: *There's always more than one option.*

She just had to find another option, and find it fast, because the Fourth of July was just three weeks away.

Emilio drove toward the home of Izzy and Ishmael Robinson's family in a defensive mood. Even the warm, rich fragrance of the pan of brownies Kitty held on her lap didn't make him excited about the evening.

For one thing, he was exhausted after the PTSD reaction of this afternoon. That much adrenaline always wore a person out.

For another thing, he couldn't relax, because he wanted to be very clear with this family. His niece was too young for any kind of connection with a boy. And yeah, he knew what Kitty had said—that boys and girls were friends at this age—but he was skeptical. Nora had had a difficult upbringing and needed a little extra protection, and he was determined to provide it.

As he drove his SUV up a long driveway, Emilio's defensiveness grew. This was the biggest house by far that he had seen in River Haven. Tall columns rose up on a massive front porch, with stone statues of lions at the corners. The lawn was as green and even as a golf course, and the gardens and shrubs were perfectly, professionally manicured. No way the twins' parents spent their Saturday afternoons doing yardwork. It would take a team of gardeners just to keep up the grounds of this place.

"Whoa, nice house," Mason said.

"No kidding," Nora said. "Ishmael said his mom's an engineer and his dad's a doctor. I guess they make the big bucks."

Apparently so. But if these wealthy people thought that a family of more modest means was less protective of their kids, they had another think coming.

The couple greeted them graciously and led the whole group to a large back patio. The twins were playing cornhole out in the grass.

"All right!" Mason said. "Come on, Nora. I can beat you, for sure."

"In your dreams." Nora followed him over to the game, holding Alice tightly by the hand. The girls probably hadn't ever been in a mansion like this. Actually, Emilio hadn't, either.

Kitty and the mom disappeared into the kitchen area, Kitty carrying her pan of brownies, the two of them chatting like old friends.

That left Emilio and the twins' father, whose name was Hank, looking at each other in a wary way.

"So I understand you have a problem with my son," Hank said.

"Not particularly, but I'm protective of my niece. She's only twelve and too young to be involved with boys."

Hank tilted his head. "Are you sure you don't have a problem with his race?"

"His race?" Emilio looked at the man, only belatedly realizing that his light brown skin and short, tightly curled black hair probably meant he was biracial. Glancing over at the twins, he realized they had features that suggested mixed race as well, although Izzy shared her mother's blond hair.

"Yes, his race. We're a mixed-race family."

Emilio lifted his hands, palms out. "That's not an issue for me. I served with men and women of all backgrounds, and believe me, on the battlefield, skin color makes no difference. Besides which, I'm darker skinned than your kids and had no idea of their race."

The other man scrutinized him for a moment, then nodded. "All right. It's a small town, and we've run into some backward attitudes here."

Emilio considered his hometown. "I can see that. River Haven isn't exactly diverse. Besides that, a few folks will consider you an outsider until you've been here for several generations."

"I've noticed that." The other man turned to the grill and checked on some delicious-smelling bratwurst and burgers. Once he flipped them, he stepped back. "I served as well," he said. "Army Medical Corps."

"Overseas?"

"Yes, but not in combat. I was stationed in Japan for a couple of years." He wiped his hands on a towel and turned back to Emilio. "So you're concerned about your niece getting involved with my son?"

"Yes. I may be overcautious, but I'm new to the parenting game, and I figure it's better to err on the side of more protective than less. My niece is only twelve. That's way too young for her to even think about dating."

"I agree with that," Hank said. "I have concerns as well."

"Yes?"

"Yes. That's one reason we invited you over. The kids say you're involved with Ms. MacIntyre. Are the two of you living together?"

"No!" Emilio kept his face blank, but inside, he was wondering what the kids had noticed. Had he let his occasional romantic feelings show?

Hank's concern felt intrusive, but if Emilio was going to question Hank's family, he guessed Hank had a right to question him. "Kitty and I are longtime friends, that's all. The girls and I are staying at her family's guesthouse for the summer. Kitty and Mason live next door."

"Okay." The other man sounded a little skeptical. "Sorry. I'm not trying to be nosy. We're just a little old-fashioned about our kids' role models. We want to encourage them to think about marriage rather than living together when the time comes. Which ideally will be far, far in the future."

Emilio had to hand it to Hank: he'd turned the tables fast. "I understand."

"I'm also…how do I put this delicately… I'm confused by the way your niece dresses. Is she in some kind of a cult?"

"No, Nora isn't in a cult!" When the kids looked up at them, Emilio realized that his voice had gotten too loud and took a breath to calm down. "She's just exploring her own personal style," he said more quietly. "To be honest, I'm not crazy about the way she dresses, either, but Kitty has advised me to choose my battles. Clothes aren't something I want to fight with Nora about, as long as she's decently covered."

"I guess that makes sense. My wife tells me to choose my battles on a regular basis." He tested the burgers again, then looked back at Emilio. "What kind of home do your nieces come from?"

Emilio had to suck in a breath to control his temper. Hank was really putting him on the defensive. He supposed the man had a right to know, given that the twins and Nora seemed to be becoming friends.

He looked over to where Nora was throwing the cornhole bag and laughing in a childlike way that made him smile. It reminded him of his sister. Emilio wanted Nora to be happy, and at her age, that meant having friends. It was worth making an effort to get along with Hank. "The girls' mother—my sister—has had her issues. She's a good woman at heart."

"But she doesn't have custody," Hank said.

"That's correct. It's a family decision— and a private one."

"I suppose I can understand that."

Soon the burgers and brats were done. The kids were called to the table, and Kitty and the twins' mother, Sydney, brought out serving bowls from the kitchen. After they all shared a prayer, everyone dug in.

As the chatter got general, Emilio decided Hank and his wife were okay. Enough that when the subject of the Fourth of July celebration came up, he was able to be honest. "I have a hard time with fireworks," he said. "We just had a bit of an episode this afternoon."

He told what had happened, keeping it light for the kids' sake.

Hank nodded. "I don't have those difficulties myself, but I've treated soldiers who do. Fireworks are a bad thing at times."

"But they're so cool," Mason protested.

"Not when the bright lights and loud sounds take soldiers back to the battlefield," Kitty said.

"Whatever." Fortunately, Mason didn't stay focused on the fireworks question. Instead, he ran out into the yard with the other kids. Dusk was falling, and fireflies flashed their little lights on and off.

Something else was flashing, too, and when Emilio looked closer, he realized the kids were playing with lighted drones. Which was cool…and was another indication that the twins lived in a different social and financial universe than the more ordinary families of River Haven.

Emilio held Alice on his lap. It was past her bedtime. She was dozing, and he gently stroked her hair, appreciating the way she leaned against his chest with trust he was still trying to earn.

Hank and Sydney started quizzing Kitty about their kids' school progress and explaining their college aspirations for them. Emilio listened, thinking. These were things he needed to start considering. Not just the day-to-day, but the future—for Nora, and eventually, for Alice.

He wasn't used to it. He'd never had a father. And his mother had been too preoccupied with day-to-day survival to think about what might be best for her children in the future.

While he had managed okay, thanks to sports, the military and the GI Bill, his sister had been hurt by the lack of parental guidance. Emilio was determined to do better by his nieces.

"Mom, did you see the drones?" Mason ran over and leaned against Kitty. "They're so cool."

"They *are* cool," Kitty said, watching the older kids as they controlled the small planes' flight patterns with handheld appliances.

"They said they even went to a drone show," Mason chattered on. "Could we go to one sometime?"

"What's a drone show?"

"Give me your phone, Mom."

"Manners. Say please." Kitty handed her phone over to Mason.

A few swipes and clicks, and Mason was holding up her phone, which portrayed a drone show, with colored lights forming into hearts and flowers and stars, and then dissolving out again.

"I've never seen anything like that," Kitty said. She studied it, tilting her head, then looked over at Emilio. "Could something like that work for the Fourth of July?

Do you think that would be better for PTSD reactions?"

Emilio leaned closer to the phone, and Mason played the video again. "I don't think they make any noise, and they don't flash in a way that resembles a firefight," he said.

"That would be so cool," Mason said. He punched more buttons on Kitty's phone and held up another video that portrayed a Fourth of July show, with light patterns of flags and liberty bells and American eagles.

"Wow, that would be an amazing solution." Kitty's eyes glowed in a very pretty way.

Emilio hated to burst her bubble, but he wasn't sure. "How much does it cost, though?"

"Quite a bit," Sydney said. She'd been typing into her phone, too, and now she showed them a number that was at least four times as high as prices they'd seen for traditional fireworks shows. "Apparently these drone shows are popular out

West, because they don't contribute to fire danger. More ecologically sound overall. But the cost is prohibitive for most smaller communities."

"Including ours," Kitty said. "Oh well, never mind."

"It's too much," Emilio agreed. He wished he were a wealthy man who could donate enough money for a show like that, just to bring back Kitty's smile.

"Oh man." Mason was disappointed, but not for long.

The kids ran off to play more, while the adults' conversation grew more general. At the end of the evening, Emilio shook hands with the twins' parents and thanked them for their hospitality.

"It was nice to meet you," Hank said. "Let's agree that these kids can be friends. I'm fine with that."

"And no more than friends," Emilio said firmly.

"Amen," said the doctor.

Kitty was looking at Emilio in a funny way, and something struck him: Being friends wasn't always as safe as he was hoping it would be for the kids. He'd seen that firsthand with Kitty.

Chapter Nine

On Saturday afternoon, the day after the cookout, Kitty received a text from Emilio.

Nora asked if you could tutor her. Willing? I'll pay you and hang out with Mason if you want. Doesn't have to be today if you're busy.

Kitty had been planning to scrub the deck this afternoon, but the rain was steady outside. Plan B was reading the mystery novel she'd started last night, and she looked at it longingly for a moment. Her couch was *awfully* comfortable.

But if Nora wanted tutoring now, it would be best to seize the moment. She really did want to help the girl. Not because she was Emilio's niece, but because she would care for any child. She was a teacher, after all.

No need to pay me, she texted back. Let's strike while the iron is hot. I'll pick her up in half an hour and we'll go down to the coffee shop.

Kitty figured a change of environment might be just what the girl needed. She talked to Mason and suggested to him that this might be a good time to work on the birdhouse that Emilio had started to help him build.

The River Runs Through It Coffee Shop was a cute place, and popular today. Situated right next to the used-book store, it was furnished with tables, comfortable chairs and a couple of couches. A mural of a river extended from one side wall to the other, across the floor, complete with images of flowers and fish and some very cute frogs. The smells of coffee and sweets filled the air, and the selection of pastries behind the glass counter looked and smelled amazing.

Kitty waved to a few students and a neighbor. After getting fancy hot chocolates and a couple of big cookies to share, she told Nora to choose a table.

She expected the twelve-year-old to go for an out-of-sight corner, in case other young people came in. Kitty knew it wasn't that cool to spend a Saturday afternoon with an adult and a teacher, even a relatively popular one.

But to her surprise, Nora walked over to the table in the window. They settled down with their drinks and cookies.

"Do you like to watch the rain?" she asked Nora. "Because this is the exact table I'd have chosen."

Nora flashed her a smile. "I do. You, too?"

"Yep. I learned to like storms from your uncle and his family."

They talked a little about River Haven, how it was different from the city. "I mean, the clothes the kids wear! Everyone looks the same. And there's no buses or taxis. If you want to go anywhere, you walk."

"That is true," Kitty said. "I lived in Pittsburgh for a while, and I liked how much there was to do." She didn't add that she'd lived there during her marriage and that there had been plenty of unhappiness during that period of her life.

"Even though it seems kind of backward here, I wouldn't mind staying in River Haven," Nora said. "Me and Uncle Emilio and Alice have been talking about it. We all like it here."

The thought of Emilio and the girls staying on permanently made Kitty's heart flutter with happiness. She didn't want to think about why.

After a little more talk, Kitty pulled up the seventh-grade curriculum on her laptop. She turned the computer around to show Nora. "Why don't you look through that and see what seems hard?"

Nora skimmed quickly through the list,

adept with the computer. Not only did the twelve-year-old seem to have decent technology skills, but Kitty suspected she was actually a pretty good reader.

Outside, the rain continued to come down. More people came in, filling the shop with pleasant chatter.

At a particular section, Nora stopped, frowning. "Writing essays is hard," she said.

"It can be. What did you have trouble with?"

Nora rolled her eyes. "The argument paper. I *have* arguments all the time, but writing them? No clue."

Kitty laughed. "Writing an argument isn't that different from having one," she said. "You make a claim and then find evidence to back it up."

"Kinda like when I tell Uncle Emilio he doesn't have to supervise me when I wanna walk two blocks to the grocery store?"

Kitty laughed. "Exactly. What evidence do you use?"

"I'm twelve years old. Mason's allowed to do it, and he's only nine. In some countries, girls my age have babies."

Kitty held up a hand. "Wait. Your first two points are good ones, but the third? You have to consider your audience. Will Uncle Emilio be thrilled to think about twelve-year-olds having babies?"

Nora frowned, and then the light dawned and she laughed. "He'd probably blow up if he thought about that."

"Right. Any other evidence you could use that would be better for convincing that particular audience, your uncle?"

"It's a small town with a low crime rate," Nora said. "Plus, people are nosy. There's always someone out on their front porch or in their yard, so if I had any trouble, I could just yell and they'd help me."

"Good!" Kitty was pleased with Nora's answer, both because it showed the girl's essential intelligence and because it spoke well of River Haven's kind people. "You're going to be fine with this. I can tell you read well, too, by the way you skimmed through that curriculum. What was the problem with English class?"

"My teacher was a stickler for rules and I missed school a lot."

Ah, attendance. That definitely would cause academic problems. "Why did you miss?"

Nora chose that moment to break off a piece of cookie and eat it. A couple of cars drove by, windshield wipers on.

"I had to watch Alice while Mom was away," she said finally.

Sensing there was more to the story, Kitty stayed quiet.

Just as she hoped, Nora went on. "Mom was away for a week when we were learning about the argument paper, and I couldn't get it done. We didn't have a computer at home to get the assignments. Uncle Emilio heard about it and got me my tablet, but it was too late."

Kitty wanted to scream, *Your mother left you, a twelve-year-old, in charge of a two-year-old for a week?*

But she didn't want to put down a woman

she didn't know. Though Nora's explanation did reveal a lot about why Emilio had ended up with custody.

"We can work on writing a little bit for the summer, but I think you'll be fine," she said.

"My grammar and spelling aren't the best, either," Nora said.

"We can work on those, too." Kitty took the computer back and started typing out a list of topics. "I'll get you some materials—worksheets and such, graphic organizers. You have to tell me if I'm overwhelming you. And you should also just read for pleasure if you have time. That really helps with English class."

"Okay." Nora looked down at her plate, then met Kitty's eyes. "If we end up staying here, I want to be caught up so I'm not in the dumb class."

Kitty sighed. She knew the kids called it that, but it was a terrible designation.

"We have two levels—level A and level B," she said. "Level A is the students who have stronger skills, and level B is the students who need more work."

"Right," Nora said. "So if I'm not in the low-level class, will I be in the same classes as the twins?"

"Probably. There are only about sixty seventh graders, so there are only two or three sections of English."

"Good. The twins are really nice." Nora looked animated, smiling in a way that showed how pretty she really was. "Ishmael says he doesn't like English much, either, but he gets good grades anyway."

"That can happen," Kitty said. "Your uncle was good at math, but he didn't like English. You heard about how I tutored him. Well, he ended up getting an A his senior year. He was so proud."

"No doubt. He's a little bit of a nerd."

Kitty smiled. "He's a good man, Nora. Be patient with him."

Nora bit her lip and looked out the window again. Then she looked back at Kitty.

"I know he's good," she said in a low voice. "He takes way better care of us than

Mom did." Quickly, she added, "Mom had a lot on her mind."

"Do you miss her?" Kitty asked. She was feeling her way. She wasn't sure how much Nora wanted to talk about her home situation, and she didn't want to push. But she thought she should open a door so the girl would know she could talk if she needed to.

"I do miss her sometimes," Nora said. "She hasn't…" Nora trailed off. She was ripping a napkin to shreds.

Kitty waited.

"She hasn't contacted us since we came here." Nora's voice was so quiet that Kitty had to lean forward to hear it. Her heart ached for the girl.

"That must be hard to deal with," she said.

Nora blinked a few times, ripping at another napkin. Then she took a sip of hot chocolate and cleared her throat. "It's no big deal to me," she said. "But it's hard on Alice."

"I'm sure it is," Kitty said. Her heart

nearly broke for the two girls. She'd had her conflicts with her own mom, but she missed her every single day. Mothers weren't replaceable.

"Have some more cookie," she said, pushing the plate toward Nora. "Chocolate makes everything better."

A smile pushed up one corner of Nora's mouth. "It does."

"I can't substitute for your mom," Kitty said, "but if there's anything you need a woman's advice on, you're welcome to come to me." Emilio was doing the best he could, but there were subjects an adolescent girl wasn't likely to want to take to her uncle.

"Thanks," Nora said. "There is one thing."

"Tell me," Kitty said, bracing herself. Even though she'd offered womanly advice, she wasn't sure how ready she was to give it to Emilio's niece.

Nora broke one of the cookies into a couple of pieces. "Can you tell Uncle

Emilio to give me more freedom and independence?"

Kitty smiled, relieved. That was easier than she'd expected. "I can talk to him about it. But you have to understand, he cares a lot. He's new at being a father figure, and he's a very protective person."

"Yeah," Nora said, "but I almost feel like I'm in prison sometimes."

"I'll talk to him," Kitty promised.

"Thanks." Nora flashed her a hesitant, sweet smile. "You're nice."

After finishing their sweets, they gathered up their things and stood.

"If you want, we can stop next door at the used-book store. I'll front you some money if you want to buy a book, and we can get your uncle to pay me back."

"Yeah!" Nora looked as excited as a kid.

Kitty's heart ached a little bit for a twelve-year-old girl, not even a book lover, who was thrilled at the chance to get a used book of her own.

As they left, she realized that she didn't feel the same about Nora as she did about her students. She felt more. She really was coming to care for the girl. She was getting involved.

It was a risk, but she couldn't help herself.

A while after Nora left to visit the coffee shop with Kitty, Alice settled down into a playdate with Juniper and Rylee. Mason was busy playing with Wyatt under Jake's supervision. So for once, Emilio found himself without kids.

He should've been thrilled. He'd thought often about how he missed the opportunity to watch a game or read a book without worrying about his nieces. But instead of relaxing, he found himself worrying about what had happened over at the fireworks guy's place.

He'd never flipped out so badly before, and to make it worse, he'd literally tackled a civilian. A very special civilian. Kitty had been kind about it, but he still wasn't happy.

He'd hurt Kitty, and that wasn't okay. It was wrong on a whole lot of levels.

First, Kitty was his good friend. Friends didn't hurt each other. Especially, men didn't hurt women physically. Although in his mixed-up brain, he'd been protecting her, the result was the same as if he'd knocked her down in anger.

Additionally, he worried about his nieces. His goal was to raise them well. But would his PTSD get in the way of that? What if it had been one of them near him when a firework had caught him by surprise? Would he have flipped out on them, shoved them to the ground? The thought of hurting Nora or Alice made his anxiety soar.

Restless with his circling thoughts, he asked Kitty's father if there was an American Legion post nearby. Learning that there was, he decided to drop by.

He showed his ID and a picture of his discharge papers and was admitted into the lounge.

Almost immediately, he wished he

hadn't come. There were probably about twenty people in the main room, either sitting around the bar or at tables. Almost every pair of eyes turned toward him when he came in.

Well, that was a small town. He nodded a greeting and ordered a soda.

As he sipped it, he wondered if he should just chug it down and leave.

Why was he even here?

The truth was, he was trying to figure out what to do about the fireworks show. Should he support it, or should he fight it? Maybe he was looking for a little support regarding the PTSD episode, too. But was he going to be able to break into this tight, hometown crowd?

A woman came over and leaned against the bar beside him. "So, you're new in town?"

"Not exactly." At least she was friendly, and he could tell from the Air Force insignia on her bracelet that she was a vet. "I grew up here," he explained.

That led to a conversation about whom

they might know in common, and the woman slid onto the bar stool beside him.

Soon she called across the bar, "Hey, Jimmy, this dude knows your cousin."

"Went to school with him," Emilio said. As they exchanged a little talk about Jimmy's cousin, the other patrons' stares and cool expressions faded.

Then the door opened again, and Mr. Wright came in. He took the bar stool on Emilio's other side.

Several of the other guys waved greetings to Mr. Wright. "Just about forgot I had a membership here until you mentioned it," the older man said.

"I didn't know you were a vet."

Mr. Wright nodded. "I served right at the end of Vietnam. Helped airlift out refugees, in fact."

Emilio waved the bartender over and pushed a few dollars forward for Mr. Wright's Coke and a refill of his drink.

Once the drinks came, Mr. Wright studied Emilio thoughtfully. "Heard you had a bit of trouble with the fireworks incident."

"You did?"

"My daughter spent time with you and came home with bruises," he said. "You better believe I questioned her."

Several heads jerked in their direction. So people were listening, even if they weren't looking at him.

One older man came over and loomed behind Mr. Wright. "No way Kitty had bruises from this guy," he said in a too-loud voice. "We don't take well to that kind of thing around here."

"Whoa, not what you're thinking," Emilio said.

Mr. Wright agreed. "He's okay, guys," he said.

But there were expectant, questioning looks, so Emilio explained how he'd gotten startled by a bottle rocket and knocked Kitty to the ground.

Several heads nodded, understanding. "Felt like you were in a war zone again, huh?" one man said.

"I've been there," another said. "Took a

lot of counseling before my wife and kids felt safe around me."

"That's a worry," Emilio admitted. "I'm guardian to my two nieces now. Afraid I'll flash back around them."

Several people nodded. The woman next to him told a story of getting freaked out with the flashing lights on a dance floor and knocking people down as she made a beeline for the exit.

One older gentleman with long, scraggly gray hair and a Vietnam Vet ball cap cleared his throat, and the others looked over toward him. He seemed to be the oldest person here, and he hadn't spoken up until now. "Kids used to follow me around with firecrackers just to watch me hit the ground," he said. "Back then, when we came home from 'Nam, there was no sympathy for vets. Nobody knew about PTSD. It was all one big joke."

"That's awful," Emilio said. But it corresponded with what he'd heard from other older soldiers.

"It's why I started drinking and drugging," the Vietnam vet said.

"You're better now?"

"Yeah." He held up his mug. "Drinking the same weak stuff you're drinking. Even go into the schools sometimes and tell my story. Fits in with Veterans Day and with the antibullying curriculum, too."

The whole place was talking now, telling each other stories. When there was a lull, Emilio spoke up to the group. "So what do you all think of fireworks displays?"

"Love them," said one of the guys, a younger vet.

"Don't bother me," his friend added.

"Me, I hide out with the music high and curtains drawn for the whole weekend," another vet said, and several nodded in agreement.

"Would you rather have an alternative celebration? I'm helping Kitty with the planning for River Haven's Fourth of July," Emilio added.

"What kind of alternative?" the woman next to him asked.

Emilio shrugged. "A movie night? Carnival? Something like that."

"Nobody's gonna like that," she said.

"Yeah, my kids won't even come if it's just another movie night," another guy said.

It was just what he and Kitty had feared. "I heard about some drone shows that were pretty cool. But—"

"I saw one of those at Disney!" one of the younger guys interrupted. "It was awesome."

"They *are* awesome," Emilio said, "but the cost is too high." When he told them the price, they whistled.

"Ridiculous," said a couple of the older guys.

"It is," Emilio said. "And anyway, private individuals would still have their fireworks."

"We should protest it if they put on fireworks," said one hippie-like older veteran.

"Nah, just party and enjoy it," someone else said.

The argument grew louder and rowdier. Mr. Wright grinned, shrugged and ordered another Coke.

"Great," Emilio said to him. "Now I've got them stirred up, but I don't have a new plan."

He did feel better that some people understood and listened. These men and women got it in a way that others didn't.

Later that night, after he had put Alice to sleep and Nora settled down reading the book Kitty had gotten her, Emilio decided he needed some fresh air.

He let Mr. Wright, Jake and Summer know that he was going out but would be nearby. They all had an agreement to help out with each other's kids for just this type of occasion, and Alice knew she could go to any of them for help. Nora, he wasn't worried about. She was planning to read a little more and then watch her favorite TV drama, and she could get mesmerized by it for hours. "In bed by ten," he told her, and she nodded without looking at him, engrossed in her show.

His bases covered, he headed out for a walk.

He couldn't deny it to himself: He hoped to see Kitty. He wanted to talk to her about what the other veterans had said. They were working together, and the vets' ideas were relevant to the celebration. He needed to let her know what he'd learned.

At the same time, he didn't want to flat out ask her to meet with him now, late at night. She'd already vetoed nighttime meetings, and understandably so.

So he strode out into the moonlight and walked slowly past Kitty's house, hoping she happened to be sitting on her porch, as she often did in the evening.

When her door opened, his heart jumped in a way that told him he just might want more than to talk business with her. But he shoved the thought away. Called out to her quietly, so as not to scare her.

She walked over, wearing cutoff shorts

and an oversize T-shirt, her hair loose around her shoulders.

Just looking at her, Emilio felt his heart start pounding.

Fortunately, she didn't seem to have the same reaction to him. "Hey, I'm glad you're out. I wanted to let you know how it went with Nora." Her voice was perfectly casual.

"Everything okay?" He tried to match his tone to hers. "Want to walk?"

She looked up at him quickly. Was she going to shut down the idea of a late meeting?

Apparently not. "I don't want to get too far away from Mason," she said. "We can do some big circles around the property if that's okay with you."

"Sure thing. Better for me to stay close, too." He didn't care where he went as long as he was with her. And he didn't even want to think about what that meant.

The moon was full in a clear sky, making the night as bright as twilight and casting a path of sparkling diamonds across the river.

They walked quietly for a few minutes. Emilio took deep breaths of cool night air and felt his shoulders relax. He liked it here. Liked being with Kitty. Life was hard at times, but good.

"So, you talked to the vets over at the Legion today, I heard. Dad said it was interesting."

"It was, and I'll tell you all about it. But first, what's up with Nora? How did the tutoring go?" Nora had seemed in a good mood when she'd returned from her afternoon with Kitty, but Emilio had figured out that you couldn't make any assumptions about the mood of a twelve-year-old girl.

Kitty smiled up at him. "The good news is that we connected," she said. "Nora is definitely smart. A little tutoring will get her plenty ready for seventh grade."

It was what Emilio had suspected about his niece. He knew from her snarky remarks that she had a sharp wit. "What's the bad news?" he asked.

"It's not really bad." Kitty squeezed his bicep for the briefest moment and kept walking.

Had the touch moved straight up her arm to her heart, the way it had done for him?

"Tell me," he said.

"It's just that she feels a little stifled," Kitty said. "I think you need to allow her more independence."

"No way," he said automatically. Nora was way too young for more independence. Didn't he already let the girl dress in ridiculous clothes and watch silly, shallow TV shows?

Kitty looked up at him, two vertical lines between her eyebrows. "Just no? No discussion?"

"That's right, there's no discussion," he said firmly. A decision was a decision. You didn't go back on it, not if you wanted respect for your authority.

Kitty kept walking slowly, looking out

at the river. Her lack of an argument made him think about what he'd said.

No discussion.

Was that what he really meant, though? Was he looking at things wrong? "I'm doing the same thing to you that I do to her," he said slowly.

That earned him a smile. "Kind of," she said. "You're a little overly emphatic about your need to be in control. Wonder why you react that way."

Again, the fact that she hadn't criticized or yelled at him made him think more clearly about her question. "I didn't have a dad," he said, puzzling it out in his own mind. "Being a parent figure to the girls is pretty new territory for me."

"I get that," she said. "And yet, you don't seem unsure of yourself. You seem to have a sense of what a parent figure should be like. A strong sense."

He thought about that. "It doesn't come from my mom. She was too frazzled earning a living and dealing with her own complicated life to give us much guidance." He shook his head slowly. "Any idea I have about authority figures comes from sports and the military."

"Uh-huh. Coaches and drill sergeants. Is that what you want to be to the girls?"

"Hey, I'm not a drill sergeant," he protested. Then, when she wrinkled her nose up at him in a very cute way, he couldn't help smiling. "Not all the time, anyway. Maybe sometimes."

"Yeah. Maybe." She was still looking up at him expectantly, waiting for him to figure it out.

No wonder Kitty was considered a good teacher. "I should probably work on being less of one."

"Probably. They're both sensitive. And young."

They walked on for a few minutes in silence. "How'd you get so smart about parenting?" he asked finally.

"I was fortunate, having both parents." She frowned, looking at the ground. "Although…"

He could tell she had something more to say. "What?"

"My mom was just…" She trailed off and waved a hand. "I'll tell you the story sometime. I think my childhood was pretty good on balance, even though there were a few rough spots."

They walked on along the grassy path beside the river. A cool breeze lifted a lock of Kitty's hair, and Emilio wanted more than anything to reach over and tuck it behind her ear.

Which would be inappropriate. Wouldn't it? Was she feeling any of the same romantic vibes he was? Would she freak out if he touched her?

He forced his thoughts back to their conversation. "I guess nobody has a perfect childhood," he said. "But I want to make my nieces' childhoods as good as possible. I'll consider what you've said about Nora."

She smiled up at him. "You're a good man." She took his hand and squeezed it, and this time, she didn't let go.

Her hand felt small and soft in his. He ran his thumb over her knuckles, back and forth.

Something achy and intense grew in his chest, some kind of longing he couldn't name. When they got to the edge of the property, rather than turning, he tugged her hand until she was facing him.

She looked up at him, and she must have seen something in his face. Her lips parted a little. He heard her sharp intake of breath.

It was like someone else took him over then, someone different from the everyday, responsible man he usually was. He ran a finger over her cheek. Touched her lips. "Can I kiss you?"

"Oh, Emilio…" The words were barely audible, a breath of air.

He didn't want to make her say no. "I know, we shouldn't," he said. But he couldn't look away from her beautiful eyes.

"We shouldn't," she said, and paused. "But I want to."

"Me, too," he said.

This time, when the wind ruffled her hair, he brushed it back with his hand. Stroked it gently down her back.

Her hair was soft, so soft. How long had he wanted to touch it?

She was still looking up at him with a question in her eyes. Waiting for him to make the move, and he was too much of a man not to do it.

He lowered his lips to hers.

Chapter Ten

Kitty had never felt anything like Emilio's kiss, there in the moonlight by the rushing river.

It was so gentle, so slow. Intense, yet sweetly restrained. Nothing like kissing her ex, who had always seemed to be in a hurry. After a moment, Emilio paused and touched her face, looked into her eyes, making sure she was good with what was happening.

That feeling of having control and a choice intoxicated her. She wrapped her arms around him, stood on tiptoe and kissed him again.

And then she was lost in the security of his embrace and the sweet longing of his kiss.

The sound of a stick cracking made them both pause and pull apart a little bit. Kitty looked toward the sound.

Nora was running away from them, toward the guesthouse.

Kitty closed her eyes and made herself snap back from romantic, yielding, soft female into a responsible adult who cared about kids. "Did she see us?"

Emilio's mouth turned down into a frown. "I think so. I'm going after her."

He squeezed her shoulder gently and then strode off, his long, rapid steps closing the distance between him and the guesthouse. He followed Nora inside.

Kitty walked the few steps to a bench and sat down, her knees suddenly shaky. Her head was spinning.

They had kissed. She and Emilio had kissed.

She'd vowed that he was just a friend.

But that kiss hadn't felt like a friend kiss. Not at all.

And Nora had seen them. Which was bad—really bad. They'd told her they were just friends. What she'd seen had made that seem like a lie. Moreover, Nora was already scarred by the way her mother had prioritized casual relationships with men over her daughters.

The last thing she wanted to do was cause more pain to Nora and Alice.

She couldn't deny that she'd loved kissing Emilio, but she had to remember that it *was* Emilio. Emilio, who was important to her as a friend. Emilio, who was going to help her fix things in town by planning a good Fourth of July celebration.

Kitty slowly shook her head. She made bad choices when love and romance were involved; she knew that. Look at the last handsome veteran she'd fallen for. She had married him, and although she couldn't regret that because she'd gotten a wonderful son, the marriage itself had been a disaster. A disaster she didn't want to repeat.

She leaned back on the bench, listening to the crickets, taking deep breaths, letting the breeze cool her warm face. Trying to forget the kiss. Wondering what was happening inside the guesthouse.

After a few minutes, Emilio came striding back toward her, and she rose to meet him.

"She won't talk to me," he said. "This isn't good." Any hint of romance was gone from his voice.

"It *isn't* good," Kitty agreed. She was worried about Nora, she really was. But she wished Emilio would acknowledge that kissing her had meant something to him. That it, in itself, hadn't been bad. That it had in fact been wonderful.

She couldn't help being disappointed that Emilio wasn't reaching out to her again, didn't seem to want to hold her.

Then, as she looked more deeply into his eyes, she saw the confusion and turmoil there. He reached for her, then pulled back.

So he did still want to share an embrace with her.

They stared at each other for a long moment as the sound of the river lapping against the bank, the lonely call of a loon, grounded them in the reality of where they were.

Grounded them in what was important: the fragile emotional state of a child.

Kitty had to help, if possible. "I wonder if I could talk to her. Would it be okay if I tried?"

He hesitated, then nodded. "Go for it," he said. "Maybe she'll talk to you more easily. I'll wait out here for a few minutes and then come up. Door's unlocked."

So Kitty walked into the guesthouse and went to Emilio's suite. Inside, she knocked on Nora's door.

Loud music blared, clearly turned up to push visitors away.

Kitty tried the door, opened it. Nora sat on the bed, her knees drawn up to her chest. She looked very, very young.

Kitty put her finger to her lips, pointing in the direction of Alice's room.

Nora cut the music and glared at her. "You didn't even ask him about me getting more independence, did you? I should never have trusted you."

Kitty went in and sat down on the bed beside Nora, keeping a respectful two feet of distance between them. "I did talk to him about that, and he's going to think about it," she said.

"You were kissing him." Nora's voice was thick with disappointment and other emotions that were harder to identify. "You said you were just friends."

Kitty couldn't deny what Nora had seen. "Things like that can happen," she said, "but we don't intend for it to go further."

"What if you get together? He won't want to pay any attention to me and Alice then. He'll leave, just like Mom did."

"He won't, Nora. This was a mistake."

Nora sat with shoulders hunched, her hands twisting in her lap.

Kitty scooted over and put a light arm

around her. "You're safe with your uncle," she said. "I would never interfere with that. I couldn't, because he's more committed to the two of you than anything else, and he always will be."

Nora didn't speak, but her twisting hands settled a little.

"You're safe, Nora," Kitty repeated. "Your uncle loves you very, very much. He won't let you down. And he won't let me come between you, even if I wanted to, which I don't."

Nora glanced sideways at Kitty, then looked back at her hands.

"Please, keep talking to him. I'd love it if you'd talk to me some, too, but you don't have to. Just don't shut out your uncle. Let him know how you feel and what you need."

Nora gave the slightest nod.

After a few minutes, Kitty left the room, closing the door behind her.

Emilio had been staring out the dark window, but he spun when she emerged. "Is she okay?"

"I think so. She's worried you'll leave her like her mom did. I told her that you and I had made a mistake, kissing, and that you're committed to her and Alice."

"Thank you," he said.

Their eyes met again, held. In their shared gaze was something Kitty had never experienced before, some higher level of communication. She could read him, and she had the feeling he could read her, too. She could tell that he had liked kissing her, that he wished it could go on, but that he knew it couldn't.

She also knew she couldn't keep staring at him without kissing him again. "We'll talk tomorrow," she said and turned toward the door.

"Yes. Tomorrow," she heard him say in a soft voice behind her as she left the suite, letting the door click shut behind her.

On Sunday afternoon, Emilio walked over to Kitty's front porch and knocked on the door.

It was a beautiful summer day. Mason

and Wyatt were throwing a ball around. Rylee, Alice and Juniper were playing dolls, with Summer supervising. Nora was down at the river with the twins, fishing.

It was a good scene. He was happy to have all these kids in his life.

He remembered being overseas, stationed for a time near a crossroads between several villages. Big family groups had passed by frequently, and he'd found himself envying their conversation and laughter, the obvious rapport that came through despite the fact that he didn't speak their language.

His own family of origin had been small, just him, his sister and his mom. He'd used to watch bigger families longingly when they had cookouts for holidays or when everyone came out to support a kid playing Little League baseball.

He still didn't have that big biological family and probably never would. But he had his nieces, and right now, they were surrounded by friends. It wasn't conventional, but it worked.

See, he told himself, *you can have this good life without having a romantic partner. So get over the thought of having Kitty in that role. Get back to being just friends.*

He knocked on her door and she opened it.

His heart started beating faster, but he ignored it. Probably just nerves about their upcoming talk. "Is this a good time?" he asked.

"Sure. Let's talk out here. I'll bring us some drinks."

A moment later, she was setting glasses of iced tea on the little table between the two rocking chairs on her porch. His glass had a slice of lemon squeezed in.

He tasted it and smiled. "You remembered I like lots of sugar."

She grinned. "I remembered something else." She set a bowl on the table. Its contents glowed fluorescent orange.

"Cheese curls!" He pumped his arm and grabbed a handful. "I won't let myself eat these most of the time, but what a treat."

She laughed. "So you're still addicted."

"I am." He crunched one down.

Who else would know how he liked his tea and remember his secret addiction to junky snacks? Kitty was so sweet. So funny, so hospitable.

So pretty.

She sat down in the rocking chair, shaking back her hair and crossing her shorts-clad legs. *Just friends*, he reminded himself. That was the point of this discussion.

Although…when she smiled at him, he couldn't help remembering how smooth her cheek had felt beneath his touch, how soft and silky her hair.

Just friends, he reminded himself again.

She tilted her head to one side, her expression confused, and he realized that he was silently staring. Awkward. He cleared his throat and got a hold of himself. "So, I figured we should talk about last night," he said.

"Right." She pulled up one knee and wrapped her arms around it. "I saw Nora was at church today. Does she seem okay?"

"She's quiet, but I think she's going to be fine," he said. "But like I said, I'm sorry I kissed you. I shouldn't have done it."

One corner of her pretty mouth curved up in a smile. "You didn't do it *to* me. We were equal participants."

Yes, they had been. And Emilio had loved that, loved her obvious enthusiasm for kissing him.

He sucked in his breath. He'd had no idea it would be so hard to focus.

He looked down toward the river, where Nora was laughing. Then over at the guesthouse porch, where Alice was chasing Rylee's kittens.

The sight of his nieces stabilized him, reminded him of his goals.

"Nora and Alice need me to be just focused on them. They've seen romantic love as a disaster, and frankly, so have I, when I was growing up. So I'm sorry, but we just can't have that kind of relationship."

She leaned a little away from him and raised an eyebrow. "Whoa. It's not like

I'm begging. I don't want a dating-type relationship, either. I've made bad choices in love. Look at my ex. I don't want to make that kind of mistake again."

Emilio opened his mouth to say, *I'm nothing like your ex. I'm a good choice.*

But he stifled the words before they came out. He *wasn't* a good choice, and this thing between them wasn't going to happen. He needed to let it die.

"Anyway. I'm staying single. I'm committed to that."

"That's good, then."

They sat, looking out across the lawn. A family of ducks walked toward the river, clucking and quacking. The light breeze lifted Kitty's hair, blew it in her face.

She pushed it back. Emilio crunched cheese curls.

"Plus," she said after a moment, "I value our friendship a lot. I don't want to ruin it with all the mushy stuff."

It was more than mushy stuff, Emilio thought. Aloud he said, "I value your friendship, too. You've been a great help about how to handle the girls."

"And you've helped me see where I was wrong about the Fourth of July." She met his eyes with a steady gaze. "I'm committed to doing it your way now. We need to have a low-key, veteran-friendly celebration, and advertise it as such. It's an opportunity to educate. What could be more patriotic?"

Grateful she was still game for a low-key celebration, he stood and leaned over, wanting to hug her. At the last minute, he backed off. *No hugging*, he reminded himself, and settled for shaking her hand.

Which was awkward, and they both laughed.

"Look, I'm glad we're friends and can discuss this reasonably," he said.

"Me, too." She stood, and again they took a step toward each other. It would have been normal to hug at this point in the conversation, but they didn't.

He stood looking at her, his heart aching with a sense of loss.

He was glad to have Kitty as a friend. That was so important. But the thought of what more might have been, if things had been different, twisted his heart into a tight, painful knot.

Chapter Eleven

After the conversation with Emilio, Kitty felt strangely shaken. So a few minutes after he left, headed to the guesthouse to take charge of the little girls for a while, Kitty walked over to the front of the place to talk to Summer.

The discussion with Emilio had gone well, really. They hadn't argued, and he hadn't pushed for their relationship to stay romantic or get more so. He wanted to do exactly what she wanted to do: break it off before it started. Go back to being friends. Just friends.

So why did she feel like there was a hole in her heart?

You wanted him to want you, she thought.

She hadn't wanted it to be quite so easy for Emilio to go back to simple friendship. She'd wanted him to express regret or to tell her that if things were different, he'd have wanted them to be together. But he hadn't. He just stuck to his script and insisted that they be friends.

Which was good. It really was good.

"Hey, want to help me with this?" Summer had a box of American flags and red, white and blue pinwheels, which she'd started putting along the walkway in front of the guesthouse. "I forgot today was Flag Day until we went to church and saw all the people had their flags out. I'm supposed to be in charge of decorating the guesthouse for holidays. How would it look if we didn't even have one flag flying?"

"You do have a lot on your mind," Kitty said. "I mean, your wedding is at the end of the week." She took a handful of the small American flags on sticks and started setting them alongside the path.

"I know! I can't wait to be married to Jake. Everything's basically done for the wedding." Summer rummaged through a plastic bin of decorations. "Who are you bringing?"

Kitty paused in the middle of setting up a pinwheel. "What do you mean?"

Summer lifted a large flag into the holder beside the guesthouse door. "Who's your date?" she asked.

"I don't have a date. You know I don't date."

"You think Gemma and I are going to let you come without a date? Even she's bringing someone."

"Who?" As far as Kitty knew, Gemma was committed to the single life, too.

"I think it's some cousin or something," Summer said. "Just bring Emilio."

"Emilio?" Kitty looked over at him. He was lifting Alice high in the air, and the other two little girls were clamoring for a turn.

He was strong and handsome, laughing, and her breath whooshed out of her. If she had wanted a man for a real relationship, it would have been him.

But they'd agreed—kissing was a mistake. "Emilio and I are just friends," she said to Summer.

"All the better. Weddings are more fun with friends. None of that icky 'when are *you* going to propose' stuff. Besides, if you invite him, I won't feel bad about him being left off the guest list."

"You couldn't have put him on the guest list. You didn't even know he was coming when you sent out the invites. And you don't really know him."

"Yeah, but he's here now. I mean, I guess I could invite him last minute, but I'd rather you bring him."

Kitty frowned at her friend. "What's really going on here?"

Summer paused in the middle of digging in the decoration box. "I'm so happy. I want you to be happy. I don't want you to be alone."

"You don't want me to be alone?" Kitty tilted her head, puzzled. "I'm not alone.

I have Mason, I have a job I love, I have friends…"

"At the wedding, I mean," Summer said. "Why wouldn't you invite Emilio, if you're just friends?"

Kitty had the feeling Summer had an agenda. But she also had a point. Why *not* invite Emilio? She watched him and felt her lips curve up into an involuntary smile. He was crawling on all fours now, with Alice on his back and Rylee trying to climb on behind her. The little girls were laughing wildly.

Such a good guy.

Summer was looking at her expectantly. "Well? Are you going to do it?"

"Sure. Why not? I'll ask him." It would be a good test of their decision to be platonic friends.

By now, Emilio had collapsed onto the ground and ordered the girls to go climb on the plastic playset. Good timing. Kitty marched over, determined to invite him despite the odd, fluttery feeling in her chest.

But before she got halfway across the lawn, Nora came running up, the twins alongside her. "Wait, Kitty," Nora said.

Pleased that Nora was being friendly rather than grouchy with her, Kitty turned and smiled at the twelve-year-old.

"The twins want me to go camping with them next weekend." Nora sounded out of breath.

"Our parents said it's okay," Izzy said, and Ishmael nodded.

"Do you think Uncle Emilio will let me come?" Nora asked. "It's four days."

Kitty looked over at Emilio. "Doubtful," she said. "Getting together with friends is one thing, but a four-day camping trip? That's a lot."

"You said you'd help!" Nora's brows drew together. "I want more independence, and this camping trip is a good start."

Kitty studied her anxious, determined face. She was flanked by the twins, one on each side, and it really was a good thing that Nora had developed a friendship with them so quickly. The twins were good kids. "I'll help you get him to at least listen," she said. "Then you can talk to him later after he's thought about it."

"Okay. Thanks, Kitty." Nora gave her a quick hug before heading back toward the river with the twins.

Kitty went the rest of the way over to Emilio.

"If you're on hugging terms with Nora," he said, "things are going better than I thought."

She smiled. "Well…hold your approval for a minute. I have two questions for you."

"Shoot," he said. He sat easily on the grass, and she sat down beside him.

"First question—would you go to Jake's wedding with me this weekend?"

He frowned.

"As a friend," she added quickly. "I don't have a date—see, I don't date. So I was hoping you'd come and get some friends off my back about my social life. No pressure, though," she added, because he still wasn't smiling or nodding.

Inside, she was hurting. Was he going to turn her down? How embarrassing would that be?

"Sure, I'll come, if it'll help you out," he said. "What's the other thing?"

No "thanks for the invite" or "that will be fun" or "I want to be with you." Kitty stuffed down her disappointment. "I want you to listen to what Nora has to say and really think about giving her more independence."

He raised an eyebrow. "Oh, yeah?"

Nora came running over. Apparently, her notion of waiting and giving Emilio time to think about it was very different from Kitty's.

"Can I go camping with the twins' family?" she asked. "It's this next weekend. Thursday through Sunday, actually, and they're going to this really cool cabin in the Finger Lakes."

"I don't think—"

"It's the wedding weekend," Nora interrupted. "The guesthouse will be swarmed with people we don't know, and we're not invited."

Emilio glanced at Kitty. He *was* invited, now.

Nora had more ammunition. She was going to be a pro at writing argumentative essays. "It's Father's Day weekend, too," she said. "That stinks when you don't have a father."

Emilio's mouth twisted to one side. It made Kitty think about how he had grown up without a father, too.

"The twins are nice. You met them, and you met their parents. They're a responsible family."

Emilio blew out a sigh and looked at Kitty. She raised an eyebrow at him. She saw that he was remembering the talks they'd had.

"I'll think about it," he said. "And I want to talk to the twins' parents if I decide it might be a good idea."

Nora frowned and sucked in a breath, like she was going to keep on arguing.

Kitty put a hand on her arm. "Your uncle took a step in the direction you want," she said. "Now you need to let it go for a bit."

Nora's lower lip stuck out a little, but then she shrugged and jogged back over to the twins.

Kitty looked at Emilio. They could have worked together so well. Not just as friends, or event planners, but as partners.

But she needed to let that thought go… and hope it didn't crop up again at the wedding they were attending together.

On Thursday, an hour before Nora was to be picked up by the twins' family, Emilio sat on the couch in the suite with a baseball game on mute. Alice was on the floor in front of him, playing with one of those five-piece toddler puzzles.

From Nora's room came music and the sound of drawers opening and closing.

Emilio had the feeling he'd made a big mistake. His stomach was in knots. He shouldn't have agreed she could go on the camping trip.

He wanted to keep his nieces close at hand. His goal was to take good care of them. So why was he sending Nora off with a family he barely knew, that included a boy who he suspected liked Nora a little too well? Was it too late to retract his consent?

He'd talked extensively with the twins' parents—about their itinerary, their planned activities, the setup of the campground. And he'd hashed it out with Kitty.

The Robinsons, experienced parents, had answered his questions patiently. And Kitty had assured him that letting kids spread their wings was a good thing. Mason had gone camping for a whole week with another family last summer and hoped to do it again over Labor Day weekend.

This was normal, he told himself firmly. Letting go, loosening control was normal.

Nora had contributed to some of the conversations. She'd told him she'd stayed alone in the apartment plenty of times, caring for Alice, while their mother was away.

Which *wasn't* a convincing argument for Emilio. He wanted to provide better supervision than his sister had done. Wanted Nora to be a kid, not a miniature adult with adult-size responsibilities.

But part of being a kid was doing things like camping trips with friends. So he'd reluctantly agreed that she could join the Robinsons' trip. Now, he was questioning himself.

Nora's bedroom door burst open. "Uncle Emilio, I don't know what clothes to bring!" Nora sounded desperate, and tears stood in her eyes.

He came over to her bedroom door. "Sturdy clothes," he said. "You'll be outside getting dirty. Jeans, shorts, T-shirts, a hoodie…stuff like that."

"I don't really have that kind of stuff," she said. She was digging through drawers, clothes strewn around on the floor. It looked like a mess to him—mostly black, some items ripped or lacy, dresses that were clearly wrong for a camping trip.

Alice came over to stand at the door of Nora's bedroom, her thumb in her mouth and her teddy bear in her arms.

He pointed at Nora's combat boots. At least she had the right footwear. "Those are perfect," he said. Frowning doubtfully, he picked up a flannel shirt. "This would be good, too."

"Are you sure?"

"Call Izzy and ask."

"She'll think I'm stupid for not knowing." Nora pawed through a drawer full of shorts and pants.

Maybe this was good. Maybe this was God's way of getting Nora to stay home.

He pointed to a pair of green army-style pants. "Bring those," he said. Then he sent a quick text to Kitty: help!

"What should I do? I don't know how to pack. Help me! You're supposed to help me!"

Emilio frowned. How did he pack for trips? "Look, think about how many days you'll be gone," he said. "You'll need clothes for Friday, Saturday and Sunday, plus whatever you're wearing today. So, bring three sets of socks and underwear."

"Uncle Emilio!" Nora hid her face in her hands, her cheeks flaming.

Emilio tried not to laugh. Apparently, even the mention of underwear was embarrassing. "You asked."

"Yeah, but…"

"Three pairs of shorts or jeans, three shirts. Some kind of pajamas. Then you'll have the basics."

She frowned, pawed through her drawers some more, and then started to stuff things into the duffel bag he'd lent her. As she got going, she began to look calmer.

Maybe his sister had always packed for the girls. Was that something he was supposed to do as a guardian? He'd figured a twelve-year-old girl could mostly pack for herself, but maybe he was wrong. "Didn't you ever pack for a trip before?"

She looked at him, her expression blank. "I've never been on a trip."

"What?"

She paused in the middle of pulling socks out of her drawer. "Mom was always going away, but we never did."

Emilio felt sadness wash over him, a big wave of it. A twelve-year-old girl who had never been on a trip? Not even a camping trip or a weekend away to visit family?

How limited his nieces' lives had been. Alice was too little to travel, but Nora? It was just sad that she'd never been anywhere.

Emilio might not be the best guardian, but he could do better than that. Then and there, he resolved to take both girls on some little trip before the summer was out.

And it was good Nora was going on a trip now. She needed to learn about having vacations, packing for a weekend away. She needed to learn that the world was a big place that offered all kinds of opportunities.

He was still ambivalent about her going

away without him, but he did see the benefit of her having something special to do.

He helped her figure out which of her shirts was most likely to work for a summer camping trip. He suggested layers in case it got cold or rainy. And he folded up the rejected shirts and stacked them, figuring that the lack of a mess would help her feel calmer, too.

After she had the basics in her duffel, Nora turned to him. "What if Mom tries to get in touch when I'm gone?" she asked. "What if she visits?"

More sadness pushed down on Emilio. "If that happens, I have the Robinsons' numbers and I'll get right in touch with them." He paused, then added, "But you know, Nora, it's not likely."

"I know," she said, her voice grumpy. She went over to Alice, picked her up and carried her to the bed. She held Alice in her lap. "I'm going away for a few days," she told her sister.

They had been through this before. They'd explained Nora's trip in clear terms to Alice. But now that Nora was actually packed, it was sinking in, and Alice started to cry.

Nora wiped her tears and hugged her, looking over her shoulder at Emilio. "Maybe I shouldn't go," she said in a low voice.

Even though he had just been wishing that she would stay home, Emilio knew he had to encourage her to go. Not let her back out because of feeling responsible for her younger sibling's happiness. "Alice will be fine, and you're gonna be fine. You'll have fun." He went over and lifted Alice out of her arms. "And me and Alice are going to have fun here. We're gonna play with the kittens and go fishing and have a cookout."

"Kitties!" Alice smiled through her tears. "I go find them?"

"Go ahead," he said. "Just stay in the guesthouse." He knew that Mr. Wright was here and would notice if Alice needed anything.

Alice took off out of the suite.

Nora stared after her. "It's like she doesn't care that I'm going."

Emilio patted her shoulder. "She cares, and I'm going to have my hands full keeping her happy without you. But she'll be okay. It's good for her to get used to you doing things without her sometimes." He put an arm around her. "You're growing up, and you're getting a more complicated life with more people in it. That's a good thing." *Especially for a kid who's never been anywhere.*

Kitty tapped on the door of the suite. "I heard you're packing," she said. "Need any help?"

She was responding to his text, Emilio realized. He'd almost forgotten he'd sent it. He'd actually done okay without her.

"Go away, Uncle Emilio. I have to ask Kitty some things." Nora shooed him out the door of her bedroom and beckoned Kitty in.

Emilio had to smile. That was fair. A twelve-year-old girl might have any number of questions about what she should take on a trip—from fashion to hygiene to beauty products—that she'd rather ask a woman than a man. Whatever it was, he had confidence that Kitty would handle it just fine.

It brought the challenge home to him: raising girls without a mother figure. He hoped he was up for it.

Outside, he heard the sound of a vehicle and went to the window. A truck pulling a camping trailer was parking in front of the guesthouse. So the Robinsons had arrived.

He tapped on the door of Nora's bedroom. "Finish up. They're here," he called.

Nora came out of her bedroom, went to the window, and squealed with excitement. Kitty was zipping up Nora's duffel.

Emilio put a hand on Nora's shoulder. "You know how to behave, right?" he said. "And part of that is, I don't want you and Ishmael going off alone, okay?"

"Uncle Emilio!"

"I mean it," he said. He reached for his wallet and pulled out a couple of bills. "Take this and offer to pay for everybody's lunch on the way to the camp-ground. Offer more than once if they say no and tell them that your uncle wants you to do it."

Nora took the money, her eyes widening. "Okay," she said, and stuffed the money in her back pocket.

"And clean up after yourself. Don't make extra work for Mr. and Mrs. Robinson." That was his own mother's voice coming back to him, from times she'd sent him off with another family or to visit relatives.

"Okay, okay." She was bouncing on the balls of her feet. "Can we go down now?"

"Yes. I'll carry your stuff." He headed downstairs with her duffel bag, behind Nora, who was racing to the front door. Kitty came along behind him and patted his shoulder. "You're doing great, Dad," she said with a smile.

He smiled back at her. Kitty understood how hard it was for him to let Nora go. Her approval felt good.

Outside, Nora and the twins were talking excitedly about what they were going to do, what they would eat, what the place was like. Izzy showed Nora an extra bicycle they'd brought for her.

Mason had been riding his own bike, but now he ran over. He listened to the twins' descriptions of the campground with obvious envy.

Emilio approached Hank Robinson and shook the man's hand. "Just to be clear, I want to make sure that Nora's properly supervised at all times," he said.

The other man raised an eyebrow.

Kitty came up beside him. "You'll have to excuse him. He's never sent his nieces off with anyone before," she said. "He's kind of freaking out."

Hank's expression relaxed. "Don't worry. Like we discussed, I'll take good care of them."

"Call me if she gets homesick, and I'll drive up and get her," he said.

Nora came over and heard the last bit of that. "Uncle Emilio!" she said, her cheeks flaming. "It's going to be fine. I'm not a baby."

"No, but you're your uncle's baby," Kitty said in a light tone.

Nora rolled her eyes and went back toward the twins, and the adults chuckled.

"I'm overdoing it, aren't I?" Emilio asked.

"You're just acting like a dad," Kitty said.

Finally, everything was loaded up, and the truck pulled off with more promises of good supervision.

As he waved and watched the taillights fade, Emilio realized his throat was tight.

Somewhere along the line, he'd become very attached to Nora. Beyond any worries he had, he would miss her.

In an odd way, her departure had made him feel more like a dad. And Kitty's reassurances made him feel like he was doing an okay job of it.

Chapter Twelve

After Nora left, Kitty looked at the little remaining group and realized she had to do something to cheer everybody up. Alice was crying, and Emilio didn't seem too far away from tears himself. Even Mason was looking blue, jealous that Nora had an exciting, outdoorsy plan for the coming weekend.

Hot sun beat down through thick, muggy air. Aside from the flies and mosquitos, everything was still. Nora would be fine, heading north to the Finger Lakes, but right here, nobody would want to spend the day outside if they could avoid it.

Emilio bent down and picked up Alice. He tickled her chin. "What're we going to do today, sweetie?"

Alice buried her face in his shoulder. "Miss Nora."

Emilio looked over at Kitty, his forehead creasing. He lifted one hand in a palm-up gesture, and she knew what he was thinking. They had planned to work on the Fourth of July celebration together, to discuss whether there was money for a couple of new carnival games he wanted to add, but that wasn't going to happen while everybody was so gloomy.

Summer came out onto the steps of the guesthouse and moved away from them to shake out a small stack of rugs. She was cleaning madly, preparing for the extra guests who would come in for the wedding this weekend.

That would be fun. A little nerve-racking to go with Emilio, but it would be festive and a very happy occasion. Kids were invited, so it shouldn't get ridiculously romantic, even though there'd be some dancing.

Suddenly, an idea of how to cheer everybody up came to her. As soon as Summer had gone back inside, she clapped her hands and beckoned the little group toward her house. "Listen up. We have something important to do today. It's a lot of work and a lot of fun."

They all looked at her questioningly.

"Summer and my brother aren't having a big fancy wedding," she said. The event would be a small outdoor gathering of family and friends, nothing formal, no attendants. That was how Summer and Jake wanted it. "But there is one very important tradition that we need to do for them—a cookie table."

"Cookies!" Alice smiled, her tears forgotten in that beautiful way of two-year-olds.

Emilio tilted his head to one side, nodding. "Come to think of it, I can remember a couple of local weddings that had pretty great spreads of cookies."

"Exactly," Kitty said. "Around here, the cookie table is a tradition, and it's always a hit. You bake a ton of cookies, and everybody eats a bunch and gets some to take home, too. We'll get a good start today. I'll get Gemma involved tomorrow if we don't have enough. I know a couple other ladies who might be willing to contribute a few dozen, too. It'll be a nice surprise for Summer and the kids."

"How will it be a surprise?" Mason asked. "Won't Uncle Jake and Summer see?"

"We'll do it at our house, and you won't tell them, or Wyatt or Rylee. Big secret, okay?"

Mason agreed, and as she'd hoped, the frowning faces had cheered up. Secrets and cookies for the win. They checked on supplies, made a quick grocery store run and then gathered in Kitty's large kitchen.

Mason and Alice stirred up batter and sneaked tastes of cookie dough. Emilio proved to be decent at rolling out sugar cookies and using the big mixer.

Soon the house was filled with spicy and sweet fragrances. After setting aside sugar cookies to cool, they made several trays of peanut butter cookies. When those came out, Mason put chocolate kisses on top of each one for a couple dozen peanut blossoms. They kept Alice busy dumping premeasured ingredients into the mixing bowl and stirring it up.

Kitty turned on music, and they all talked and laughed as they worked. Mason showed Alice how to frost the sugar cookies in the pastel, wedding-appropriate shades Kitty had mixed up.

After a couple of hours of baking, though, Mason and Alice's attention flagged.

"Mom, can we go watch TV?" Mason asked.

"Watch TV," Alice echoed. She was looking up at Mason with hero worship in her eyes.

There were more cookies in the oven, but clearly, the kids were done helping. Which was understandable. It was a big project. "Can you pick out a video or a show that's okay for Alice?" Kitty asked Mason.

"I will. Come on, Alice." He took the little girl's hand and led her into the living room.

Kitty smiled after them. "They're cute together. Mason is really enjoying having Alice around. I think he was a little jealous of Wyatt having a little sister."

Then she frowned. Mason was never going to be a big brother, and definitely not to Alice. She hadn't meant to imply that.

She changed the subject before Emilio could process what she'd said. "Let's do some work on the Fourth celebration, in between finishing up the cookies. You said you found some more games to include?"

"Yeah, if we can afford them," Emilio said. "Can we use your laptop?"

She grabbed it, and they sat down together, looked over the budget and slotted in two more games.

"It's still light on a finale that brings

people together," Kitty said, skimming again through their outline.

"We could end with a movie, I guess," Emilio said.

"That again? We already decided movies probably wouldn't work." Out of desperation, Kitty pulled up a list of Fourth of July movies. After looking over the titles, they both shook their heads. "I don't think we can find something that everybody will like," Kitty said. "I mean, some patriotic movies are pretty intense. But the kids' ones won't keep the adults entertained. And we definitely don't want to show something political. We want everybody to be happy."

"True. How about a battle of the bands?"

She winced. "That's another area I don't feel confident about. There's a group of high school kids that want to play, and I told them they could, but truthfully, they're not that good. Maybe we could add in some professionals."

"Not a battle of the bands, then. It wouldn't be a fair contest. We could have the kids play first, and then end the evening with the pros."

"That could work. I like it."

"If we can find a band that'll come last minute," Emilio said.

"We can. We have to." Kitty knew of a few people she could call. "How about amping up the food, too? In addition to the grilling, we could do a community potluck. That'll get more people involved."

"Food safety laws?"

Kitty frowned. "Could be a problem. I mean, we do potlucks at church, but I don't know about a bigger event."

Emilio was tapping computer keys. "It looks like if we're not charging for the food, guidelines are more flexible."

"We have extra funds because of skipping the fireworks. We don't have to charge for food." Kitty made phone calls and found a couple of possibilities for bands. She also got in touch with some women who were skilled at running potlucks for funerals and other events at the church, and they quickly agreed to help organize a community potluck on the Fourth.

"I just want people to have a great time. With no negatives, like last year." After all, the reason she'd taken charge was to prove that she and Mason weren't like her ex-husband.

"Yeah. I'm sorry you have to think about the whole fireworks thing. Planning your event would've been a lot easier if I never got involved."

Would it? Kitty thought about it, tried to imagine doing this on her own. Even though that had been her original intention, and even though she'd have probably found a way to include a fireworks show of some kind, she wasn't wishing Emilio had never come. Now, she could hardly fathom putting the event together without his input. "We're a team," she said. "We're in it together, for better or worse."

He gave her a narrow stare and nodded, and only then did she realize she'd just quoted a piece of the wedding ceremony to Emilio. Her face heated.

"Let's pray about it," he suggested. "We'll pray for a celebration that meets everyone's needs."

"And that everyone enjoys." That he'd even suggested prayer warmed Kitty's heart.

They held hands, and each of them asked for help in arranging a meaningful, fun celebration that would work for everyone, kids and adults, civilians and the veterans and animals who found fireworks bothersome.

Emilio's voice was a deep rumble, and his hand clasping hers felt large and warm. Kitty couldn't help imagining what it would be like to fall in love with a man whose faith was as deep as hers, maybe deeper. A man who wouldn't mind sharing a leadership role in a family's spirituality.

That was a huge mistake she'd made in her marriage. She had paid more attention to superficial things, looks and attraction and fun, rather than depth of character and a shared faith.

She'd paid the price for that. She wouldn't make the same mistake again.

When their prayer was finished, they looked at each other and smiled. It took a minute for them to drop each other's hands.

She hadn't expected this problem: that their domestic day, working and praying together, would deepen the feelings she was already starting to have for him.

But maybe she was wrong to call it a problem. If they could work together, and play together, and pray together…was it possible that they were made for each other? That being together wouldn't ruin their lives, but rather, make them better?

All that night, Kitty's heart raced with possibilities.

Emilio walked over to Kitty's house on the Saturday of the wedding. Alice was in the crook of his arm, dressed in a cute little sundress.

His heart pounded as if this were an important date, but he kept reminding himself: It wasn't a date. He needed to keep it in the friend zone with Kitty.

Unfortunately, his heart hadn't received that memo.

Mason came running out of Kitty's house and down the porch steps, wearing khaki pants and a button-down shirt. "Mom! They're here!" he called back over his shoulder. He ran to Emilio and held up his arms for Alice, and Alice struggled to get down. She was well on her way to developing a crush on Mason, if two-year-olds could have a crush.

He set her down beside Mason and then looked up as Kitty came out the door. He sucked in his breath.

She wore a loose, floaty sundress, pink with flowers on it, her suntanned shoulders bare, her long hair curling around them.

Friend zone. Friend zone.

He smiled and held out a hand to her as she came down the steps. "Ready, my lady?" he said, keeping his tone light and joking.

She laughed. "Ready, fine sir."

"This is the easiest trip to a wedding I've ever done," he said, making conversation to keep his mind off how pretty she looked. "They didn't want a church wedding?"

"Well, they both love the outdoors, so they decided to have it here by the river, where they fell in love." She glanced up at him just as he was looking over at her. Something about her words—*falling in love*—clutched at his heart. "Don't worry," she went on quickly, "there'll be a minister and vows and everything."

Alice and Mason were running down toward the river, where rows of white chairs were set up in front of an arched wedding arbor covered with flowers. Nice.

"Jake and Summer are all about simplicity," Kitty went on. "They're building a house, and they wanted to save for that, too."

"That makes a lot of sense." It was what Emilio would probably choose, too, if he were to get married.

Which was *not* in the plans.

They strolled down to where people were gathering on the riverbank, probably about forty guests from what Emilio had heard. A string quartet started playing, and everyone took their seats.

As Kitty's date, Emilio sat right up in front with the family. It felt like family, too. Mr. Wright, old-fashioned, was wearing an actual suit, one of the few guests who was. Mason sat beside him, then Kitty, then Emilio, then Alice. Alice quickly climbed into Emilio's lap to see everything better.

Jake and Summer didn't have regular attendants. Instead, Summer's kids, Rylee and Wyatt, went down the aisle. Rylee scattered flower blossoms, and Wyatt carried a box with the rings.

And then the music shifted, and everyone stood to watch Jake and Summer come down the aisle together.

Summer kept looking up at Jake, smiling, cheeks pink. Jake put an arm around her and dropped a kiss on the top of her head, crowned with a wreath of flowers. They looked radiant, joyous.

Could that ever be him?

Even though he wanted to keep things in the friend zone with Kitty, he couldn't help imagining himself in Jake's role as a groom, a husband. The simple, beautiful ceremony made him think about the family he'd always longed for but didn't believe he could have.

Marriage wasn't the norm in his family. His mother and dad hadn't been married, nor had his sister married any of her boyfriends. They had no wedding traditions. But ever since he'd become a Christian, almost ten years ago now, he hadn't wanted to just have unofficial or transient relationships. If he did start a family, he'd want to be married, committed to his wife and to any kids that would come of the union.

Alice wiggled in his lap, and he thought about the fact that having custody of his nieces would play into whether he actually got married or not. A lot of women wouldn't want to take on a ready-made family. Although Nora and Alice were doing well, raising them was still a challenge and would continue to be.

Kitty wouldn't mind.

He thought about that as he stood beside Kitty, watching the rest of the ceremony. He was attracted to Kitty—there was no denying that played a role—but it went deeper now. They worked together well, and she was helping him become a good father to his nieces. Already best friends, they were becoming more like family.

And yet, he and his nieces were only here at the Holiday Haven guesthouse for the summer. He and the girls had agreed that they wanted to stay in River Haven. But staying right here at the guesthouse next door to Kitty? That couldn't last.

No matter how much he wanted it to.

Friend zone, friend zone.

Romantic love ruined the good stuff, didn't it? That was what he had always thought. That was how it had gone in his own family.

But looking at Jake and Summer as they said their vows, seeing their obvious joy, he had to admit that there were some exceptions to that rule. Jake and Summer sure seemed like they were going to have a happy life, despite—or because of—the romantic love they felt for one another.

He looked over at Kitty, who was wiping a tear as the ceremony ended. "You okay?" he whispered to her.

"Just happy," she said. "Happy, and a little sad. I'm not exactly losing my brother, but it feels that way, sort of."

He didn't mean to put his arm around her. It just seemed to happen. He wanted to cheer her up. That was all, wasn't it?

No. The truth was, he wanted to hold her. To comfort her. At the very least, to dance with her at the reception. Could he do that and still stay in the friend zone?

Kitty felt happy and excited and all in a flurry.

She was thrilled for her brother, and glad she could be here today to support him and enjoy his happiness. She wasn't going to worry about the Fourth of July celebration, nor about Emilio. Not today.

Emilio… As he walked beside her and Mason, toward the reception area, she couldn't help glancing over at him, again and again.

He wore charcoal-gray slacks and a white button-down shirt with the sleeves rolled up. His deep tan was obvious and looked great on him. He had a muscular build that seemed to be shown off in dress clothes even more than in casual ones.

But even more than how good he looked, she liked the way that he kept an eye on Alice and talked kindly to Mason. He stopped to pick up a baby's shoe and hand it to the parents who were walking ahead of them. He helped Mrs. Matthews, who used a cane, over a rough patch of ground.

He wasn't just centered on himself the way a lot of men were. He looked out for others. He had a touch of the caretaker's gene in him, and he wore it well. How had that happened, that a man who'd lived a tough, macho life as a soldier could also wipe a toddler's tear with perfect tenderness?

A jazzy band was setting up on the big deck, which had been cleared of most of the furniture to allow for dancing later. On the lawn, long tables covered with pink-and-white-checkered tablecloths held food of all kinds. Off to one side was the table supporting the wedding cake, and next to it, the cookie table that she and Emilio and Gemma had put together.

"Hey, you're the people I want to see," came a voice behind them. It was Mrs. Michaelson, one of the busy moms who seemed to have a finger in every pie in town. "I wanted to ask you about the Fourth of July celebration. I heard a rumor there won't be any fireworks. Is that true?"

So much for not worrying about the Fourth of July today. "Yes, that's right," Kitty said, straightening her spine. Beside her, she felt Mason tense.

"Why on earth are you not having fireworks?" Mrs. Michaelson asked. "Everybody loves them so much."

"Well, part of the reason is that the group I originally hired had to cancel," Kitty said.

Emilio spoke up before she could continue. "I'm mostly to blame for the decision not to find and hire another fireworks producer," he said. "As a veteran, I struggle with PTSD. Kitty has seen how fireworks affect me, and it's not pretty. And I'm not the only one, so we decided together to go with a different kind of celebration."

Mrs. Michaelson raised an eyebrow. "Together?" She looked from Emilio to Kitty and back again, her eyebrows slightly raised.

Oh, great. Let the rumors start. Kitty had better speak up, and fast. "Yes, when I was putting together the celebration, I realized having the input of a veteran like Emilio—a decorated combat veteran—would be really valuable to make sure we're recognizing the kind of event a Fourth of July celebration should be. And he really did give valuable input. I hadn't considered the negative impact of fireworks until talking with him about it."

"Humph. If you think that's the right decision." She walked away, shaking her head.

Emilio glanced down at Kitty. "She didn't sound too happy."

Kitty tried to laugh. "Come on, let's not worry about her. Let's enjoy the wedding. Starting with the cookie table."

Gemma stood behind it with her cousin, who was her date for the wedding. "Look how well it all turned out. Everybody's raving about the cookie table. We did good!"

Indeed, people were coming over, commenting on the cookies, tasting a few for now and expressing happiness that they could take a bagful home at the end of the event.

Gemma pulled Kitty aside. "You and Emilio look good together. Anything happening in that department?"

"No," Kitty said firmly, aware that she was also trying to convince herself. "I mean, you and your cousin look good, too, but it doesn't mean you're having an exciting romance."

"Touché," Gemma said. "I'm a strong single lady and I mean to stay that way."

"Me, too." Kitty held out a hand.

Gemma shook it. "Deal. I'm glad to have a no-romance rebel like you around. Because Summer and Jake are making it all look pretty good."

In fact, Summer and Jake did look very happy as they circulated among guests. Summer's long white dress was a casual summer style that suited her perfectly, and Jake wore a summer linen suit. Working in the auto repair business, he rarely dressed up, but when he did…wow. Her brother was super handsome. She was so proud of him.

When she saw him talking with their father, she excused herself and went over to join them. The three of them shared a big embrace.

"I wish your mother were here," Dad said. "She'd have loved to see you happily married."

Kitty glanced at Jake. They were still dealing with the discovery of what their mother had done. But it hadn't killed their father's love for her. He was such a forgiving, good person.

When their father walked away to greet an old friend, Kitty gave Jake another hug. "I'm so happy you're happy," she said.

"I really am." Her big, tough brother actually had a tear in his eye. "It's so amazing that I found Summer. And I can't believe how fortunate I am that she wants to stay right here and build a life in River Haven."

"The two of you are perfect for each other," Kitty said. "And I'm so, so glad you're going to stay close to me and Dad."

The wedding reception went on, with plenty of eating and drinking and dancing. And Kitty did dance with Emilio, as well as with Jake and a couple of other friends.

She had to be honest with herself: It

felt a little special dancing with Emilio. Maybe a lot special. Feeling his arms around her, breathing in the clean, woodsy scent of him, noticing the beard stubble when their cheeks brushed together…all of it swept her away.

She tried to stifle that feeling. She was still so scared of moving their relationship past friendship.

Finally, they all sat down. Alice climbed into Kitty's lap and rested her head against Kitty, and Kitty hugged her and felt a tug. She wished this were her daughter. If anything would develop between her and Emilio, she would gladly take on his nieces, love them like a mother.

As the sun set, she looked from Emilio to Mason to Alice with an ache in her heart. This wouldn't go on forever. This closeness was just for the summer. It wouldn't last.

But she had to admit, she wished that it could.

Noise up at the guesthouse caught her attention. Car doors slamming. Shouting.

Not happy, jolly shouting, but upset shouting. She looked over at Emilio and stood, holding Alice. "What was that?"

He stood at the same moment, frowning. "Sounded like Nora."

They hurried toward the guesthouse, Alice in Kitty's arms and Mason tagging along, and walked around it to the front entrance.

Nora was pulling her bags out of the Robinsons' truck, crying.

"Nora, are you okay?" Kitty asked, rushing to the girl. "We didn't think you were coming back until tomorrow."

The twins' father came around from the driver's side. His eyebrows were pulled together in a frown. "We tried calling but didn't get an answer," he said. "We came back early because Nora and Ishmael couldn't follow the rules."

Uh-oh. What had they done?

Chapter Thirteen

Emilio put a hand on his sobbing niece's shoulder. "What happened? Is anyone hurt?"

Kitty stood beside him, holding Alice on her hip. Mason stood next to her. Hank and Sydney Robinson had gotten out of the truck, and now Hank beckoned to Ishmael, who climbed out and stood beside his parents, looking wretched.

From behind the guesthouse, the sounds of music and laughter came, faintly.

"No one's hurt," Hank said. "But I'm pretty upset with Nora and Ishmael. They sneaked off from a picnic we were having with a couple of other families." He paused and glanced at Alice, then Mason. Apparently, what he had to say wasn't fit for young ears.

"Run down and ask Grandpa when they're going to cut the cake, will you, hon?" Kitty asked. "Take Alice with you."

Mason nodded. "Come on, Alice, race you!"

Kitty put Alice down, and she toddled after Mason, yelling, "Race, race!" The two of them disappeared around the side of the guesthouse.

When Mason was out of earshot, Hank cleared his throat. "We found them kissing."

"What?" Emilio's pulse rate sped up and heat flashed through his body. His hand tightened on Nora's shoulder. "I told you not to be alone with Ishmael."

Nora twisted away from him and crossed her arms over her chest. Tears were still running down her face.

"Exactly right," Hank said. "They were told they needed to stay with the group, by us as well as you. It was dangerous of them to go off by themselves in the woods."

That part hadn't even occurred to Emilio. Visions of snakes and bears and steep rock drop-offs played through his mind. Anything could happen to a couple of green city kids alone in the woods.

Anything could happen to a vulnerable young girl who was willing to go with the first boy who showed an interest. She was like a little prey animal thrown into a den of dangerous lions. Didn't have a chance. Just like her mother hadn't had a chance.

He'd been wrong, wrong, wrong to let her go.

A better person would have kept her close to home, safe with him. That had been his first impulse, but he'd let himself be persuaded to loosen his hold on her. And look what had happened.

He was flawed as a guardian, horribly flawed. He'd grown up in a home without good safeguards for kids, and against his will, that was the kind of environment he'd created for Nora.

"We were only gone half an hour," Ishmael said. He was staring at the ground, not meeting anyone's eyes.

Even through his anger, Emilio could see himself in the boy. He wasn't as much to blame as the adults were.

"Because we came looking for you," Hank said. "Both of you know you're too young for that kind of relationship." He looked from the pair of kids to Emilio. "So the consequence is that we all came home."

"Yeah, thanks for ruining our camping trip, you two." Izzy, who must have been listening through the truck's open window, yelled the angry words from the back seat.

Nora cried harder.

Emilio's head was spinning. He couldn't believe the disaster he'd feared had happened. He should never have let Nora go off with this family. He glared at Hank. "You said you'd supervise them."

Sydney straightened beside her husband. "We're sorry about that. We thought they were mature enough that we didn't have to watch them every moment, but we were wrong."

She sounded upset. Hank sounded upset, too. But not anywhere near as upset as Emilio felt. Neither of them seemed to see this for the disaster that it was.

"Let me know if you want to talk more about this," Hank said. He reached out a hand, and reluctantly, Emilio shook it. "I'm sorry the camping trip had to end this way," he said to Nora.

Nora looked up at him and choked out, "I'm sorry we broke the rules."

And then the Robinson family climbed into the truck and drove away.

Emilio's thoughts churned. Why had he let her go away? Now she'd started down a pathway that Emilio knew could lead her to disaster. The same pathway that his own mother—and Nora's—had followed.

"What were you thinking?" he asked

Nora. "I told you not to go off alone with him."

"Don't yell at me!" Nora covered her face with her hands, her shoulders slumping, sobbing.

Sweat dripped down Emilio's back. His face felt hot. "You're in a heap of trouble, young lady."

Kitty put a hand on his arm. She didn't say anything, but he felt in the gesture her desire to restrain his anger.

Nora turned and ran into the guesthouse.

"You go straight to your room," Emilio called after her. Then he turned to Kitty. "You! You talked me into this."

Mason came around the corner of the guesthouse, holding Alice's hand. "They're cutting the cake in ten minutes. And people are getting their bags of cookies."

Emilio needed to get control of himself. He didn't want to scare the kids. He held out his hands for Alice, and sweet little thing that she was, she let him pick her up.

After a couple of deep breaths, he spoke

to Kitty in what he hoped was a calm voice. "You said she needed independence. Obviously, you were wrong. She couldn't handle it. I would think as an experienced parent, you would've known that."

Mason stepped between Emilio and his mother. "Stop yelling at my mom," he said. "It's not her fault!"

"I'm not—" He broke off. He wasn't yelling, but maybe he was speaking a little too loudly and harshly.

The boy's protective stance made Emilio stop and think, though. Of course Mason would defend his mother, but maybe the kid was right. Maybe it wasn't Kitty's fault.

Kitty put an arm around Mason. "Thank you, honey." She drew him a little closer, as if she needed comfort.

"Want cookies," Alice said, struggling to get out of Emilio's arms.

"Do you want to take Alice down to get her own bag of cookies?" Kitty asked her son. "You can get a bag for us, too."

"One for each of us?" Mason bargained.

"Of course. After all, we baked most of them." She smiled at her son. Her voice didn't even sound upset.

"Come on, Alice, let's get some cookies," Mason said.

Kitty looked up at Emilio, raising one eyebrow. "If that's okay with her uncle," she said in a perfectly flat tone. Which made him realize she was, in fact, very emotional. She was just good at concealing it in front of her child. That was a parental skill Emilio obviously needed to work at.

"Can she?" Mason looked up at him. Both his expression and his voice were guarded. Kitty hadn't fooled him, obviously; he knew there was something going on between them.

Emilio nodded, and the two children walked off hand in hand.

After they disappeared, Kitty faced him. "I don't appreciate you blaming me. We discussed about whether to let her go because we're friends—at least, I think we are—but you made the final decision."

He stiffened, feeling it as an accusation. What right did she have to accuse him, when she'd been the one to argue for more independence for Nora?

But he shouldn't try to pass the buck. "You're right, and I'm sorry. It's not your fault. It's just that, without your input, I'd never have let her go."

"Okay," she said. "That's fair. But Emilio…kids make mistakes and get in trouble. It's not the end of the world."

Anger rose up in him again, a red wave of it. "It could be the end of her world," he said, aware that he was speaking too loud again but unable to stop himself. "She's heading in the same direction as her mother."

Kitty shook her head as if he were being unreasonable. "She's twelve and she kissed a boy."

"That's how it starts!" he yelled.

Kitty rolled her eyes and lifted her hands to the sky. "That's ridiculous. You're way overreacting."

"That's better than not reacting! Are you saying I should just let this go?"

"No, of course not. She needs a punishment. But she already got one. She had to come home early. Can't you see how bad she feels about that?"

"She's never seeing that family again!"

"Emilio." Kitty reached out to touch his arm.

Just because he wanted the comfort of her touch so much, he yanked it away. He didn't deserve comfort.

This was what happened when he went soft and romantic. He'd ruined everything with his niece through his own bad judgment.

Images played in his mind: his mother, sobbing over some man who'd done her wrong. His sister, telling him she was pregnant and that she didn't even know for sure who the father was. Poverty. Bad choices. Drinking. Neglecting your kids and losing custody.

He had vowed he wouldn't let his nieces go down that path, but he'd been swayed by his own romantic feelings into listening to Kitty's mixed-up views.

"I need to go speak with my niece," he said.

"If you want, Mason and I can watch Alice while—"

"No." He took a deep breath and let it out slowly. "I've let myself depend on you way too much. As of now, I won't be leaning on you for parenting help."

Kitty wilted a little, her forehead creasing.

A round of laughter rose up from the wedding reception. They were missing the cutting of the cake. A joyous moment she should experience with her family, but he'd wrecked that, too. All of this was affecting Kitty's life, and not in a good way.

"Are you backing out of helping with the Fourth, too?" she asked. He could tell that she was trying to control her tone.

Part of him wanted to pull her into his arms, to hug and comfort her and get comfort himself.

But that was what had got him into trouble in the first place.

"I'll help you," he said. "But let's limit our contact. Things have gotten too intense between us, and that can't happen anymore. It warped my judgment and…" He waved a hand at the guesthouse where Nora was. "I'm very concerned about the consequences."

Kitty was looking at him with those beautiful eyes, now wide and hurt. "You *are* blaming me," she said.

"I'm blaming myself," he corrected. "And I'm blaming whatever this is between us that distracted me from my goals."

"I see." She nodded and looked down at the ground.

From behind the guesthouse, music swelled up again. A car drove by on the road with a friendly honk. A couple of guests came around the guesthouse and walked toward their cars.

Kitty was just standing there looking forlorn, and it nearly broke his heart.

Half an hour ago, they'd been dancing together. He'd loved having her in his arms. He'd let himself imagine what it would be like to be with her more like that, to marry her, even. He'd gotten carried away with romantic fantasies.

But romance ruined everything. He'd known it, but he'd forgotten it for a little space of time.

He'd ended up hurting her, this woman he'd known from childhood. He should have protected her better, too.

He faced her. "Look," he said. "Maybe someday we can be friends again."

She looked up at him. "We're not even friends now?"

His heart ached. His whole chest ached. "We need to take a break from that."

Mason and Alice came around the side of the guesthouse. Alice ran to him. "Look, cookies!"

He knelt to look at the little bag she was carrying. Then he picked her up, needing the solid comfort of holding her.

Alice babbled on about the cookies. That

made him think of how they'd baked them together. The fun, the domesticity of that.

He had let it get out of hand, and now there was a bad result.

"Are you two still fighting?" Mason asked.

"No, kiddo." He reached out to ruffle Mason's hair, then stopped himself. He couldn't be as close with Mason, either, not now.

He met Kitty's eyes, big and hurt and stormy. It was hard to look away.

She pressed her lips together. "Okay then," she said. "Come on, Mason, let's go home." Without another word, she turned and walked toward her house. Mason followed behind, looking puzzled.

Slowly, Emilio walked into the guesthouse, feeling more exhausted than he had after the worst firefights he'd experienced in his years overseas.

Just get through today, Kitty told herself the morning after the wedding.

Mechanically, she got ready for church.

Needing to keep busy, she fried bacon and made pancakes.

Mason, being a nine-year-old boy, ate enthusiastically. But after he gobbled down his own stack of pancakes and crunched through about ten pieces of bacon, he looked at Kitty with worried eyes. "Is Nora in a lot of trouble?" he asked.

"I don't know," she said. "I think so."

"She probably is, if she's the reason they had to come home from their camping trip early," he said, tilting his head to one side. "What did she do?"

"Not our business," she said. "Hurry up and finish. We're leaving for church in fifteen minutes."

As Mason finished his pancakes—and then hers, since she had no appetite—she realized that she'd spoken the simple truth.

It wasn't her business. Nora wasn't, and Emilio wasn't.

As of now she was fired. As a parenting consultant. Even as a friend.

And it went without saying that there

was no chance of anything more between her and Emilio, not now.

She sat through the church service beside her father, trying to let the Scripture and the music and the message wash over her and sink in.

She couldn't quite pay attention, but the familiar ritual soothed her. During the time of quiet prayer, she begged God for help.

Help Emilio find the right way to resolve things with Nora. Help me quit hurting. Help me give up on him, let go, move on.

That wasn't going to be easy. Definitely impossible without some divine assistance, because just seeing Emilio across the sanctuary felt like a punch in the stomach.

She was hurt, but she was angry, too. Wasn't it just like a man to lay it all at her feet? Something had gone wrong, and immediately he'd shifted the blame from himself to her. And then he'd rejected her, shoved her away.

She had made a mistake letting him get too close, thinking something could work.

Her lungs constricted, making it hard to breathe. Cycling back and forth between hurt and anger, she lost track of the service until the closing music swelled up.

As she was heading toward the exit, looking for Mason, several people came over to her. Word had spread, apparently, that there would be no fireworks at the Fourth of July celebration.

People were not happy. Her father's buddy asked if it was true, and when she confirmed it, just walked away shaking his head. One of the oldest ladies in the congregation told her how excited she'd been about seeing the fireworks with her great-grandchildren. When Andy Archer, a professor at a nearby college, started lecturing her about patriotism and community needs and the history of Fourth of July celebrations, she blew up. "I know that, Andy, okay? I'm doing the best I can!"

She spun away so she wouldn't start

crying or lashing out at everyone. As it was, people were glancing her way and murmuring.

Part of her anger was that she felt like the professor was right: The celebration would be out of line with what it should be historically.

It didn't help when Mason told her he'd experienced similar criticism in Sunday school. "People say it's going to be no fun at all, Mom," he said. "Can't we have fireworks?"

It was too late to set anything up at this point. All the fireworks companies were no doubt booked. Besides, she'd made a commitment to a quiet celebration, and she wasn't going to go back on it. "No, honey, we can't."

He shrugged. "Just thought I'd ask," he said. He ran off to talk to one of his school friends. Even at his age, he knew when to push an issue with his mother and when it was a better idea not to. Smart kid.

She walked out onto the church lawn, where people lingered, talking and laughing. The sun was shining, and the air felt warm and fresh. One of the women's groups was offering up coffee cake and lemonade. A group of people cooed over a new baby.

Everyone was having a great time, uplifted by the service and the beautiful day. Everyone but her.

She saw Emilio walking toward his truck, his nieces at his side, and another wave of anger rose in her. He should be at her side, fielding questions and lending that combat-veteran authority to her decisions about the event.

Now she had to deal with this alone. She had to *limit contact* with him. After all she'd done for him.

She watched him hold the door for Nora and then buckle Alice into her car seat, and despair washed over her. She had loved helping him learn to take care of the girls. Had admired how warmly he'd taken to parenting. She felt for Nora and wondered whether she and her uncle had managed to work things out.

But she couldn't know, might never know, because he had cut off contact. Pushed her away and slammed the door.

She felt terribly, terribly alone.

Wanting to leave before she broke down and made a complete fool of herself, she looked around for her father. She spotted him and headed over, then stopped. He appeared to be having a great time, chatting with people about the wedding and listening to congratulations on his son marrying a fine woman. He seemed oblivious to the situation between her and Emilio as well as to any controversy about the Fourth. Which was good. He didn't need to worry about her problems.

She couldn't turn to her brother. He was on his honeymoon with her good friend and half sister, Summer.

She had no one.

When Gemma walked toward her, holding Juniper's hand, Kitty hailed her like she was a lifeline. Maybe she was.

"What's wrong?" Gemma asked.

Kitty opened her mouth to tell her friend

what was going on and then stopped, because she couldn't choke out any words. Her eyes filled with tears.

Gemma put an arm around her and led her farther away from the after-church crowd. "Is Mason going to the go-kart place with the church kids this afternoon?" she asked.

Kitty had lost track of everything, so she checked her phone. "Yes, he's going."

"Then I'm leaving Juniper with Emilio and we're going out—you and I."

"I don't think that's going to work. He's…not in a good mood."

Gemma shrugged. "He can get over it. He owes me. I'll pick you up at two."

As Kitty collected Mason and headed with her father toward their vehicle, she clung to that promise. She'd never needed the counsel of her wise friend more.

Chapter Fourteen

Emilio climbed slowly into the driver's seat of his truck after church, feeling weighted down with responsibility. He had to put the girls first, raise them right. The trouble was, he didn't know what *right* was, not at the moment, anyway.

Nora sat beside him, but she wouldn't look at him, and her eyes were rimmed with red. Alice, picking up on her sister's mood, was fussy and discontent. She'd started crying for her mother in the middle of the night, and she hadn't completely recovered today.

Emilio had hoped they could all feel better by going to church. He, for himself, hoped to get some spiritual perspective. Hoped to figure out how to do the right thing.

It hadn't happened in church, partly because of Nora's miserable presence beside him and partly because of worrying about how Alice was doing in the nursery.

He'd talked to Nora for a little bit last night. Not so much to scold her as to understand why she'd done what she'd done. She hadn't exactly opened up to him, but she'd let him know that she was distraught about ruining the Robinsons' camping trip. She was sure that Izzy hated her for it.

Emilio was almost relieved to know she cared so much about what Izzy thought. She'd barely mentioned Ishmael. Maybe they weren't deeply involved, not yet.

He had hugged her, told her they would talk more about it and that he still loved her and always would. He could only hope his words would sink in at some point.

The other reason he hadn't found peace

in church was that he'd seen Kitty, gorgeous in one of her flowered sundresses but looking tired with dark circles under her eyes.

In the midst of his anger at her—which he knew was misplaced—he felt guilty. Kitty had done a lot for them, and although he had to back off from her, he knew he'd been unkind in how he'd gone about it.

All of it churned inside him. He was about to pull out of the parking lot when he spotted Pastor Kevin walking across the grass toward his parsonage next door.

He stopped the truck. "Be right back," he said to the girls. He got out and jogged over to the pastor. "Any chance we could set up an appointment to talk sometime next week? I'm having some troubles, and I could use your perspective to help me figure them out."

"I actually do house visits," the pastor said, smiling. "Even on Sundays."

Wow. Emilio swallowed. He hadn't expected the pastor to be quite so available, and he wasn't sure he knew what he wanted to say to the man.

"There's a condition," the pastor added. "That we meet outside, on the Wrights' dock, and do some fishing while we talk."

Ah. Emilio had heard that Pastor Kevin was an avid fisherman. And having an activity would take the pressure off their conversation. He'd see if Mr. Wright could take care of Alice for an hour or two. "That would be great," he said. "Come on by whenever you're ready."

Later that afternoon, they toted lawn chairs down to the river. The pastor had brought his own fishing gear, and Emilio had borrowed some from Mr. Wright's large stash.

It was an overcast, muggy day—perfect for fishing, according to Pastor Kevin. He'd brought a bucket of minnows. Emilio had only ever fished with worms—he couldn't claim to be much of an outdoorsman—but he watched and followed Kevin's lead.

The process transported him back to childhood. He hadn't had a dad to teach him to fish, true. Growing up in a river town, though, friends and their fathers had filled some of the gap.

They tossed their lines in the water. Emilio listened to the waves lapping against the shoreline, felt the slight breeze on his face, and watched an osprey swoop down toward the river, looking for its dinner. Slowly, a measure of peace washed over him.

After a few minutes, Emilio explained what had happened with Nora and Ishmael on the camping trip.

When he was finished, the pastor nodded slowly. "I can see why you're upset, but kids make mistakes," he said.

That again. Why couldn't anyone understand that this was serious? "Kitty said the same thing," he told the pastor, "but you guys don't get my family. This is our slippery slope."

"Your mom's and sister's, or yours,

too?" The pastor's shrewd eyes seemed to see into him.

"Good question." He reeled his line in and tossed it out again, getting it out farther this time. "I do have feelings for someone," he said slowly. "But no intention of following up on them."

"Why not?" The pastor jerked his line out of some weeds. "And by the way, I'm pretty sure I know the identity of the woman in question."

Great. It was obvious. "Because romance ruins everything," he said.

The pastor raised an eyebrow. "Everything? For everyone?"

Emilio reeled in his line and knelt to rebait his empty hook. "For my family, at least. For me."

"How's that belief working out for you?"

Emilio didn't answer, but he thought about it. It *wasn't* working. He was miserable. And yet, it was the only way to be safe.

The pastor's rod jerked and bent downward, and he stood. "Got me a fighter here." He let the line out and reeled it in again, a fish pulling and jumping and splashing.

"Looks like a big one!"

"Net him for me?" Pastor Kevin gestured toward the net.

Emilio grabbed it and, after a little more struggle, managed to get the big rainbow trout into the net.

"That's dinner," the pastor said. He put the fish on a stringer and let it down into the water.

After they'd settled back into their chairs, Emilio's mind returned to the situation with Nora. "I get that everyone makes mistakes," he said, "but why did Nora do this, and at such a young age? Is she already headed down the same path as her mom?"

"One mistake doesn't define her any more than it defines you," the pastor said. "Maybe they were just experimenting. Maybe they did it because they knew it was forbidden."

Emilio froze. "You're saying I pushed

her into it?" How could that be? He was trying to set the right boundaries, tracks inside which the girls could safely move forward and grow. But if those very boundaries had caused Nora to veer outside…

The pastor shook his head as he reached for a sinker. "I'm sure it's more complicated than that. Have you talked to her about it?"

"Just a little. I told her I still loved her and always would."

"Good man. That's the most important thing for her to hear."

Emilio felt his shoulders relax. He'd gotten that right, at least. "I told her she couldn't see the twins anymore, but… Will that push her into his arms, too?"

The pastor shrugged. "No way to know in advance. How do you feel about that punishment?"

"I don't know." Emilio let his head sink into his hands. Mostly, he felt confused. About everything.

"Maybe give it a time limit instead

of forbidding her to see the twins ever again," Pastor Kevin suggested. "After a little while, you might allow them to do something supervised together, with your families."

"Am I wrong for worrying?"

"Nope. Kids grow up fast. You definitely want to keep an eye on those two if they're really drawn to each other now."

Emilio's bobber ducked, and he reeled it in, feeling excited. But it turned out to be just a clump of weeds. He cleared the hook, baited it again and threw the line back out.

Birds sang around them, and a family of ducks swam past. The sun peeked out from behind the clouds. A gentle breeze swept away some of the humidity.

Pastor Kevin was pretty smart, encouraging a meeting outdoors. Doing something fun, in a beautiful place, definitely had made Emilio feel better. He needed to do more of this.

"I've seen it before," the pastor said thoughtfully.

"Seen what?"

"Sometimes it happens that you meet the love of your life while you're a kid. Some of our happiest marriages in the church are that way."

Instantly, Emilio flashed on a vision of Kitty as a child. He had loved running through the woods with her, swimming in the nearby lake while their mothers sunbathed, defending her on the playground. It was pretty special to know what she had been like in school, to know her family and her background so well.

What if that was going to be the case with Nora and Ishmael? Would he deny that to his niece?

"I knew your mom and sister a little," Pastor Kevin said unexpectedly.

"You did?" Emilio was surprised. "We weren't churchgoers when I was growing up."

"They came for a stretch when you were small," the pastor said. "Everyone noticed. Your mom and your sister were real beauties."

The thought of his mother going to church, of the ways that could have influenced her life had she stuck with it, made Emilio sad. Same for Bianca. "I feel like my sister is a lost cause. She abandoned her kids. It's hard to get past that."

"There's always redemption," Pastor Kevin said. "Your sister may turn things around. But…you're prepared to keep the girls?"

"Yes. I'm committed to raising them. I'd love it if my sister would come back into their lives, but I'm their rock and their home, and that's how it's going to stay."

"Good man." The pastor nodded approvingly.

They fished for a little while longer.

Emilio turned it all over in his mind. Finally, he spoke up again. "You really think people like my sister can change, be redeemed?"

"Always," the pastor said with quiet confidence.

"Can the girls forgive her?" he asked. "Can I?"

"I think so. You know the Lord's Prayer—'Forgive us our trespasses, as we forgive those who trespass against us.'" He looked at Emilio sternly. "Don't forget the second part of that. We forgive those who trespass against us. Which happens all the time. Bianca trespassed in a major way. Nora trespassed, less seriously. You need to forgive her. And you need to forgive yourself."

"I'll keep that in mind," Emilio said. Inside, he was thinking: How about forgiving Kitty? Who hadn't even really trespassed against him?

He, in fact, had trespassed against *her* with his harsh words and cold treatment.

Would she ever forgive him?

After another half hour, Emilio stood. "I better get back to my nieces," he said. "I told Gemma I'd watch her daughter for the next couple of hours, and I need to keep an eye on Nora. You're welcome to stay and fish into the evening if you want."

"I just may." Pastor Kevin smiled. "Nothing like fishing to clear your mind."

"Fishing, and some good advice. Thanks

for this. I feel better, like maybe I can actually talk to Nora in a decent way."

"I'd be glad to talk to her, if you like, but I think it would be better coming from you." The pastor looked thoughtful. "Maybe we could get her to come to some of the youth group activities. It might help if she had a broader circle of friends than just the twins."

"That's a good idea. I'll look into it."

"And Emilio. Listen to your heart."

He nodded and shook the pastor's hand, then walked back up toward the guesthouse. He let Mr. Wright know that he was back, and the older man headed down to do some fishing with the pastor.

Emilio thought about Pastor Kevin's parting words. *Listen to your heart.*

If he did, he knew what it wanted. It was yearning for Kitty, his old friend, the girl next door.

The woman he loved.

Kitty and Gemma arrived at the Sweet Hills Berry Farm late Sunday afternoon.

If anything could have cheered Kitty up, this had to be the place, just half an hour away from River Haven. Groups of people shopped or sat around small tables on the covered patio, talking and laughing. An open-air market was loaded with blueberries, raspberries, jars of jam, pies and small gifts. The surrounding fields alternated between berry bushes and gorgeous pink peonies, available for cutting.

The place seemed lively and fun, but Kitty was feeling anything but festive.

She'd seen Emilio talking to the pastor down at the river, fishing. Had seen them get excited about a fish one of them was pulling in. *Great*, she'd thought. *Have a wonderful time. Glad you're getting yourself some new friends since you dumped me.*

"Thanks for bringing me," she said to Gemma as they headed from the car to the patio area, trying to inject some enthusiasm into her voice.

Gemma laughed. "I can tell you don't

want to be here, but just look! We can pet a donkey!"

"Pet a donkey?" Kitty hadn't expected that, but sure enough, they were passing a small petting zoo area. Children were inside one section, running around chasing lambs and other animals. Kitty and Gemma walked up to another section, where a friendly donkey looked out over the fence.

They petted its velvety nose, laughed at a cranky goose that was chasing a goat and then walked into the food area.

"See," Gemma said, "I just wanted to show you that it's a big world with lots of people in it. And there's a whole world outside of River Haven."

"And donkeys," Kitty said. "Good to know."

The truth was, she didn't want to meet a lot of new people. And she didn't want to be outside of River Haven. She wanted Emilio, or she'd thought she did. But he'd made it clear that she couldn't have him.

Her melancholy was like a film on top of

the anger that kept bubbling up to the surface. In her head she knew she shouldn't feel angry, since Emilio was just trying to do the right thing for his nieces. And kids always came first. If she were a better person, she'd text Emilio and let him off the hook, tell him it was perfectly fine that he'd blamed her and dumped her and left her high and dry.

But she couldn't do it. She'd used up all her "it's okay, honey" cards on her ex-husband. There were none left for Emilio.

Which was why she shouldn't be in a relationship, any more than the nasty goose in the petting zoo should find a mate.

They ordered pie and ice cream and then found a table. "Tell me what happened," Gemma said.

"You sure you want to hear it?"

"Of course I do!"

So Kitty told her friend about planning the new and improved Fourth of July event, and baking cookies with the kids, and dancing at the wedding. How it had seemed like something might actually work between her and Emilio.

And then how Nora had come home from the camping trip early and everything had blown up.

"So…he blamed you?"

"Yep. After a little while, he said he didn't. But he still wants to back off all of it. Even our friendship." Her throat tightened up on the last word.

"That's really rough." Gemma stood and hugged her. "Let's go pick up our pie, and we'll figure out what to do."

They carried their pie and ice cream back to their table, along with cute little coffee drinks. A vocalist and guitar player filled the air with quiet music. Lush green vines surrounded the seating area, muffling the sound of people talking and laughing.

"Let's pray fast," Gemma said. "We don't want our ice cream to melt. God will understand."

That made Kitty laugh. They quickly

thanked God for the day and their friendship and the food, and then dug in.

Warm blueberry pie. The sugary, flaky crust, the explosive sweet-sourness of the berries, the cool ice cream…all of it filled Kitty's senses. After several bites, she put her fork down to rest and savor the richness. She smiled at Gemma. "This does make me feel better," she said.

"Told you so. Listen to Aunt Gemma."

After they finished their pie, she looked across the table at her friend. "I don't think we can solve the Emilio problem," Kitty said, "but the other problem is the Fourth of July."

"I thought everything was pretty much in place."

"It is. But there are no fireworks, and everyone's mad about that. I did it for Emilio, but…"

"But now he's being a jerk." Gemma tilted her head to one side. "Are you thinking of changing your mind and putting on a fireworks show?"

"No." Kitty shook her head. "He *is* being

a jerk, for sure, but I still won't do fireworks. I didn't realize how bad it was to have them."

"Yeah. Lots of doggos hate it, too. But aren't you having music, dancing, a potluck? What's not to like?"

"People are still complaining. Even hassling Mason about it."

Gemma's face creased with distress. "Oh no. Is he upset?"

Kitty shook her head. "He seems to be taking it in stride. More than I am."

"What if we add a pie-baking contest? I think we've established that no one can be sad when there's pie around."

"Good point," Kitty said, laughing. "But…that's a lot to organize. I don't know if I can manage one more element. It's already complicated."

"I'll organize it," Gemma said promptly. "It's a way to help."

"You're a good friend," Kitty said, meaning it.

"Hey, ladies." The deep voice came from above them, and Kitty looked up to see two men standing there. One was dark-haired, and one was blond and balding. "Mind if we sit down?"

They were a little old for Kitty and Gemma, but they seemed polite.

And Kitty had no interest at all. A glance at Gemma ascertained that she wasn't dying to get to know these guys, either. "Thanks," Kitty said, "but we have some talking to do."

"Oh, come on. You ladies look lonely."

"No, really. We have things to do."

"Can't they wait? We'll buy your drinks. Or more pie. You can afford to eat it—you're both slim, not like some of the ladies here." The blond man puffed out his cheeks and held his arms out in mockery of an overweight person.

Kitty nearly let her head flop down onto the table. Why, oh why did she attract every loser in the county?

Gemma raised an eyebrow at Kitty and then addressed the men. "First of all," she said, "I noticed that you're judging women's figures. Not men's. Only women's."

She looked pointedly at the blond man's pot belly. "Acting like a mean seventh-grade boy is no way to make women like you."

"And second," Kitty chimed in, "you didn't listen to what we said or respect our judgment. You stuck around even when we said we had other things to do. So. No, thank you."

"What's wrong with the two of you?" one of them asked.

Kitty rolled her eyes. "Because obviously, your lack of success is our fault."

"Run along," Gemma said, waving the back of her hand at them.

"And for your next conquest," Kitty added, "you might want to find some better pickup lines."

The men slunk off, and a woman who'd been sitting within earshot leaned over to high-five them. Her tablemates applauded.

They all watched as the two men left the seating area and headed for the parking lot.

"They're actually leaving," Kitty said, amazed. "We really ruined their day."

"Yeah, and I don't feel even a little bit bad about it," Gemma said.

They started giggling, and then giggled some more, until it was hard to stop.

Finally, Gemma managed to speak. "See? There are plenty of fish in the sea!"

They laughed a little more.

"Rough fish," Kitty said, "but yeah." An image of Emilio and Pastor Kevin fishing from the dock flashed into her mind. This time, it didn't seem as painful. She could imagine that if Emilio had seen her and Gemma clowning around, he'd have thought she was insensitive about what had gone down between them.

They finally settled down and leaned back to listen to the music. Beside the eating area, a bouncy house had attracted kids, who were shrieking with joy.

"Boy, they're cute," Kitty said. "Makes me wish for more. I always wanted a sibling for Mason."

"I get that," Gemma said. "I would love

to have a sibling for Juniper—if it didn't involve men."

"Well…" Kitty said doubtfully, "it doesn't have to involve men. You could adopt."

"And you could, too, for that matter," Gemma said.

They looked at each other. "Maybe," they said at the same time, then laughed again.

But adopting without a spouse wasn't what Kitty had in mind. "Thing is," she said, "I'm kind of hooked on Emilio."

"That's fair," Gemma said. "He seems like one of the good ones. Sure better than those losers." She pointed in the direction the two unpleasant men had gone.

"He is. I've known him forever, and there's nothing bad in him. He's a combat veteran, and he's committed to raising his sister's children. He's a great guy."

"But…" Gemma said.

"But he doesn't want to be my friend." Kitty sighed. "I should have known. I never do well in love. I mean, look at my ex. Another handsome vet who treated me badly."

"Now wait a minute." Gemma raised her hand, palm out. "There is really no comparison. I've met Jeff. He's *not* one of the good ones. He lied to everyone."

"Yeah, which is what got me into this whole Fourth of July thing in the first place. Trying to prove my patriotism, but I think it backfired."

"You know, Kitty, this town knows you're not like Jeff. Mason isn't, either. People may have made a few comments, but everyone's going to end up on your side."

"Maybe," Kitty said. "I guess I feel concerned because people keep coming up to me and asking about the celebration. Some have even asked me about whether Jeff will be there."

"They'll get over it," Gemma said. "Besides, who cares what people think?"

Kitty smiled at her friend. Gemma, with her quirky hairstyle and clothing, definitely didn't care much what people thought. In a way, she reminded Kitty of her unconventional mother.

And she'd been kind and insightful this afternoon, just like Mom had been on her best days.

"You're a smart lady. And thanks for this."

"I wish I could fix it." Gemma patted her arm, an expression of sympathy on her face.

"Your friendship means a lot," Kitty said. "And I do feel better."

It was true, she reflected as they left. She had so much to be thankful for. Her faith and church family. Her beautiful son. Work she loved. Her dad and brother and Summer, her new sister. And friends. Good friends who helped her feel strong without a man.

"I'm going to buy a pie for Dad and Mason to enjoy," she said, and they veered over to stop at the little market on their way out.

Normally, she'd have gotten enough for Emilio to share it, and he'd have loved it.

Blueberry pie was a favorite of his. But no. She wasn't reaching out to him. Not if he was going to cut her off. Let him come to her if he wanted to.

Chapter Fifteen

On Monday night, Emilio asked Nora to come sit with him on the screened porch at the side of the guesthouse. He didn't want to pressure her too much, but he did need to talk to her. Partly to rebuild his relationship with her, and partly to make her see the error of her ways.

So he told her that it would be a cool place to watch the storm that was coming in, and her face lifted a little bit from the scowl it had fallen into when he'd approached. He, his mother and his sister had always liked storms, and he was counting on the fact that his sister had passed that on to her girls.

She had. Some fresh popcorn and cold soda finished the deal, and soon they were out on the porch as darkness fell and the rain started to splatter down.

The cool breeze that came in matched Emilio's cooled-down feelings. He wasn't angry at Nora anymore, not really. He knew he had been too harsh with her. But he was also still worried about her. He wanted to find out where she stood and whether he needed to do more to make her understand her mistake.

He held out the popcorn bowl to her and then spoke. "First off, I want to apologize."

Her eyebrows shot up. Apparently, she'd expected him to lead with another scolding.

"I came down too hard on you. I want to talk it through. But first, how are you feeling?"

"Bad," she said flatly. "My life stinks." She didn't look at him as she said it, just looked out at the rain and the faint flashes of lightning far away.

Well, he should've expected that attitude from a twelve-, almost thirteen-year-old girl. They were nothing if not dramatic. "You want to tell me more?"

She looked at him like he was foolish for even asking. "My mom abandoned me, my uncle hates me, my little sister is freaking out and now I'm forbidden to see my only friends. Even my tutor is avoiding me."

"Whoa." When she put it that way, he understood. She wasn't just being dramatic. He studied his niece, so tough, so defiant, so wounded. She'd had way too much to deal with in her short life. He wanted to make things better for her, but he was utterly confused about how. "That does stink."

"I know, right?"

"Is Alice really freaking out?" he asked. He'd spent time playing with his younger niece today, and she had seemed okay. Perky and sweet, in fact. He said as much.

"Yeah. I think… Well, she's afraid

you're gonna leave us like Mom did. So she's trying to be extra good."

Oh, boy. The thought of little Alice trying to hold in her two-year-old emotions made him terribly, terribly sad. "Did you tell her I won't leave?"

"Won't you?" Nora crossed her arms over her chest and lifted her chin. Behind the sharply spoken words and rebellious posture, he saw something else.

Fear. Nora thought he'd leave them, too. He leaned forward and held her gaze. "No. I won't. You have my word. Just try to get rid of me. You can't."

Her mouth twisted to one side and she looked away, blinking a few times. Some of the stiffness left her shoulders.

Suddenly he wondered whether certain parts of her behavior were about that: testing him to see if he'd leave.

Well, he wouldn't. Emilio hadn't always been the best student, but that was one test he was determined to ace.

The rain was coming down harder now,

the flashes of lightning closer. Thunder boomed in the distance.

He reviewed her list of problems in his mind. "I don't hate you, Nora. Anything but. That's why I got so upset, because I want the best for you."

"Really?" She looked skeptical.

"Really. One hundred percent."

"So, you think isolating me from my friends is the best?"

He smiled and shook his head. "You know what? You're good at arguing."

"I am." She flashed a half smile. "That's what Kitty said, too."

Kitty. Emilio couldn't stop thinking about her—what he'd said to her, her reaction, the way she was avoiding him. He'd like for her to be here with them, watching the rain, talking to Nora. Was she out on her porch now too? She'd hung out at his house during several storms back when they were kids. Liked them, it seemed.

But he couldn't focus on Kitty and himself and his own problems here. He thought back over Nora's list of challenges and attacked another big one. "As for your mom… I'm really sorry about how she's acting, what she's doing. I hope we hear from her soon, but…" He spread his hands in a "who knows" gesture.

"Do you think we will?" Nora asked it in a low voice. Didn't look at him at first, then shot him a glance.

"I don't know. She's being very unpredictable. But one thing I do know—it's not you girls' fault. She had some bad experiences. Made mistakes that, well, they kind of damaged her, and that's why…" He trailed off, studying his niece's profile, wondering how much to say. He wished parenting came with a guidebook. Wished he could have talked to Kitty before having this conversation, gotten her advice.

Nora looked at him. "That's why what?"

"Why you kissing a boy freaked me out," he said. "Your mom got going down the wrong road due to her relationships with men, and I don't want you to do the same."

"I kissed one boy!" Nora sounded indignant. "And barely," she added thoughtfully. "I didn't even really like it."

He looked over at her, raised an eyebrow.

"I just wanted to try it, okay?"

Relief washed over him, fresh as the rainwater that dripped from the eaves. She hadn't liked it. She wasn't yearning for more. Still, he felt he needed to remain stern. "You went against my rules and the Robinsons' rules. That's not okay."

"I know, I know, I'm sorry." She looked at him full in the face. "I really am. I shouldn't have done it. I hate that I caused the camping trip to end." She frowned. "Izzy was so mad at me."

"She's not anymore?"

Nora shook her head. "Not so much."

Lightning cracked and thunder boomed. The storm was right overhead.

"How do you know? You weren't to have contact with either twin."

She widened her eyes, making her expression innocent. "I wasn't to *see* them. You didn't say anything about texting."

He let his head sink into his hand. Oh, man. If she was like this at twelve… He turned his face to the side and looked up at her. "Have you been texting with Ishmael, too?"

"A little," she said. "It's actually kind of awkward."

Another relief. This wasn't serious passion. This was a couple of shy, inexperienced middle school kids making their first stab at a boy-girl connection.

Sympathy twisted at him as he remembered some of his own early attempts at dating. "It can be awkward," he said. "Or it can be great." He stopped there. In no way was he ready to talk to his niece about the ins and outs of kissing and dates and young love. She really needed a female confidante.

"I wish I could talk to Kitty," she said, echoing his thoughts.

"You can. I don't think she's mad at you. She's mad at me."

Nora tucked her legs under herself. "I

tried texting her. She says she can't meet with me unless you say it's okay."

"It's okay. Of course it's okay."

"Well, you have to tell her so. And I guarantee she's not gonna be happy with you. You were hard on her for something that wasn't her fault."

Wisdom from a young mind. "You're not wrong," he said.

They sat, watching the storm, crunching popcorn. After a while, Nora went inside to get two more cans of soda. She didn't seem to be in a hurry to escape, and that made Emilio happy.

He stared out into the darkness. To raise his nieces well was his goal, but he was learning there was no set of rules, no obvious answers. There was complexity to it, shades of gray. He needed to really talk with the girls, not just tell them how to behave.

When Nora came back, he tried to explain some of that. "I didn't have a father," he said as he opened his can of soda. "I had some mistaken ideas about what a father, or a guardian, ought to be. I thought they were supposed to be always sure of themselves, passing down orders that were then obeyed. But in reality, fathers make mistakes and so do kids."

She was pouring her own soft drink, so she wasn't looking at him, but he could tell she was listening.

"I made a mistake when I got so mad at you, Nora, but I'm still worried."

"Because of Mom?"

"Yeah."

She studied him and then looked out at the rain. "I wanted to be like her when I was little. She was so pretty and glamorous. Everybody loved her."

"She was." He remembered his sister in younger days—her hair curling down almost to her waist, her makeup perfect, her manner charming and bubbly. The last few times he'd seen her, though, she'd seemed nervous, a little haggard, more manic than bubbly. "How do you feel about her now?"

"I don't want to be like her anymore. I would never want to do to a kid what she did to Alice and me." She frowned. "Me, maybe I deserved it. I was mean to her sometimes, mouthy. But Alice is just a baby. She never did anything wrong, and Mom left her anyway."

Her words made Emilio's chest hurt and tightened his throat. "You didn't deserve it, and you didn't do anything wrong. You were just being a kid." As he said it, he realized that both Kitty and the pastor had made a similar claim about the kissing incident. Interesting.

"So," Nora went on, "if kissing boys leads to being like that—which I doubt, by the way—I think I'll hold off for a while." She treated him to a sassy look and an eye roll.

"Especially since you didn't like it that much," Emilio dared to joke.

She made a wry face at him. "Rub it in, will you? But yeah. I'm too young. We're both too young. We agreed about that."

"When you were texting without my consent," Emilio said.

She raised a finger and shook it back

and forth. "Without you forbidding it, either."

"Only because I didn't think of it."

"That's on you, old man." She grinned at him.

His heart felt like it was expanding in his chest. Growing three sizes, just like the Grinch. Nora had expressed some fears and he'd been able to address them. Now she was joking with him. Maybe, just maybe, they were back to the relationship they'd begun to build. Maybe talks like these would make it even stronger.

How he loved this feisty child.

Nora's expression went serious again. "You and Kitty wouldn't have fought if it wasn't for what I did. You were good together. How are you gonna fix it with her?"

Great. Nora had seen that there was more than friendship between them. His niece was scarily insightful. Plus, he had to admit, they'd given fuel to her suspicions. Nora had caught them embracing a couple of times. "I want to fix it," he said, "but I don't know how. And I want to help her make the Fourth of July celebration great, but I'm one of the reasons she didn't try to get a new fireworks vendor. She saw me have a PTSD episode and realized why fireworks are tough on vets."

"She decided to go a different direction, and now people are mad at her for it." Nora nodded thoughtfully.

They watched the storm for a few more minutes, munched popcorn. Then she sat up straight. "I think I might have an idea…"

Kitty had become accustomed to texts from Emilio during the past week. Businesslike texts about the Fourth of July plans. They barely bothered her.

When she heard a knock on the door, opened it and found him standing there, though, that was something different.

He looked uncertain. It was a hot day, midafternoon, and his forehead shone with sweat.

Immediately, her heart started pounding, angry and hopeful and hurt.

She raised an eyebrow but didn't open the door.

He spoke through the screen. "Look, I just… We've had so many texts, I figured we should just talk over last-minute details in person. Plan the week." He paused and studied her. "Unless you don't want to."

"No, it's fine." Although it wasn't. Didn't he realize he should've texted her asking if it was okay to meet, not just shown up?

He was still looking at her, his head tilted to one side. "You okay?"

"Just not sure how to act when we're working together, but we're keeping a distance and we're not friends." Hurt words, but they were honest. She *was* hurt.

"Look," he said. "I realize now I was way too harsh."

"You think?" Rather than inviting him inside her home, she grabbed her tablet and came out to the front porch. "Fine. Let's get this work done."

It would be useful, for sure, to finalize everything in person. Make sure they each knew what they needed to do in the last week before the event. But how to do that without getting too emotionally involved, that was the question. Being with him, even for the few seconds they'd been together, was painful. She couldn't help finding him attractive as he bent over the tablet, reading through the list of last-minute tasks.

Couldn't help inhaling his clean, soapy fragrance.

Grrrr. Scold herself as she might, she couldn't help being drawn to this man.

"Looks like we have the potluck covered," he said in an upbeat tone that sounded a little forced.

"Yep," she said.

"And the pie-baking contest is a great idea. Do you think it should be a pie-eating contest, too?"

She frowned. "Too late to make changes. The festival is in one week."

"Oh! Sorry. I… I had one other change to suggest, but…"

"What is it?" she asked, sighing.

"To have a couple of the older veterans speak. If you don't want to, it's okay."

He was being so deferential. Looking at her so nervously and then glancing away.

Somehow the tables had turned, and he was afraid of her. And it wasn't very noble of her, but she liked the feeling of power.

"Having the veterans talk sounds nice," she said. "We can do it before the dancing, at nightfall."

"Good! I'll talk to them." He looked like he was about to say something else, but he didn't.

"Are you going to speak about your experiences, along with the other vets?"

"No." He shook his head. "I'm not good at it. I'm more behind the scenes."

She remembered that about him, remembered coaching him before some of the presentations he had to give in school. The memories almost drew her into feeling close to him, but she resisted the emotion.

Mason came banging out of the house. "Hey, Mom?"

Something in his voice made her look up sharply. He sounded worried. "What's up?"

"Dad called." He was shifting from foot to foot, biting his lip.

She couldn't help tensing a little. Her ex called Mason periodically, and they were slated to spend some time together over the weekend of the Fourth. There was no reason to feel nervous, but she did.

"I told him we were in charge of the Fourth of July celebration this year." Mason looked at her, then away.

"That's okay. You're allowed to talk to your dad about whatever you want."

"Yeah, but Mom…he said he might come."

"What? No. That's not okay." All the blood rushed to her head, and cold sweat gathered on her neck. She was working so hard, trying to make the town celebration great so as to get past her ex's bad legacy, and he wanted to show up? Ruin her efforts?

"Just to pick me up," Mason said quickly. "I think, anyway."

She glanced at Emilio, automatically hoping for reassurance. He was paying attention. Not getting involved, but alert.

"Your dad's picking you up on July 5," she said to Mason.

"Yeah. But he said he might come early."

Kitty hesitated. She didn't want to say bad things about her ex. Not in front of Mason. But Jeff's presence could ruin everything. "I'd rather he didn't," she said. "He upset people last year."

"I know!" Mason flopped down on the steps and wrapped his arms around his legs. "I didn't know how to tell him not to come. I'm sorry."

Kitty scooted down to sit beside Mason. She hated, hated, hated this aspect of divorce. Even when you tried hard not to bring your adult conflicts to your kids, they felt them, were affected by them.

"Don't worry. You didn't do anything wrong. I can call him and talk to him."

"No, it's okay. I'll just put it all on you." He flashed her a grin. "I'll tell him you said not to come."

After Mason had run into the house, Emilio looked at her. "Disaster averted?"

She let out a breath. It *would* have been a disaster if her ex had come, and there was nothing she wanted more than to talk to Emilio about it. They were at odds, and yet, he was someone who would understand.

"Yeah," she said. "That's the last thing we need."

"It'll be fine," he said with certainty. "The celebration we've planned will block people's memories of last year."

She wondered how he could be so confident. "Probably not completely. I hope it mostly will, though."

Their eyes met, and some kind of wordless communication passed between them. Something about the past they had as friends, and the promise they had felt together recently, and then the distance Emilio had imposed.

It was awkward, and Kitty wanted to cry. She forced herself to lift her chin and be at least a little peppy. "How's Nora?"

"Better," he said. "We talked. Thanks for meeting with her, tutoring her."

"Of course." Kitty had enjoyed meeting with Nora a couple of times last week. They had talked about school and had mostly avoided the topic of the twins. "Her, I have no problem with."

"Right." He met her eyes again, then looked away. "Well, I better take off, then, if we're done."

"We're done."

He walked down the stairs, glancing back at her once.

The whole experience left her feeling emotionally involved, not detached as she'd hoped. Also very confused. Why was he being so gentle, so nice, but not addressing the issues between them?

Chapter Sixteen

Emilio and Kitty worked together smoothly, if a little awkwardly, in the week before the event. Fortunately, almost everything was done, because Emilio had to set his apology plan in motion. That was going to take some time and fancy footwork.

He really hoped his idea—or rather, his and Nora's idea—worked out.

Saturday the Fourth arrived all too quickly, and the events they'd planned began to unfold. River Haven's downtown park was decorated with flags and banners and balloons, and multiple stations invited people to play games, dunk River

Haven's unofficial mayor, learn about the church, eat delicious food—some of it grilled on the spot and some of it brought in as part of the potluck—and judge the pies. There was a temporary stage off to one side of the park, where the high school music group alternated with a talented three-person band, playing patriotic songs, traditional and contemporary.

Tonight, Emilio was basically in charge of troubleshooting. When a tent started to collapse, he fixed it with help from Jake and Mr. Wright. When a little boy lost his mother, he announced the boy's name and comforted him until his frantic parents could be found.

Kitty was everywhere, giving directions, organizing things, in her element.

Emilio was conscious, always, of where she was. At first, he tried not to focus on her, and then he gave up. He couldn't keep his eyes off her, in her red shirt and cutoff denim shorts, her hair in a long ponytail tied with a red ribbon.

He noticed every detail about her, down to her red, white and blue toenail polish.

A few people questioned him about the no-fireworks decision, but not many. Kitty had taken a brilliant step, snagging an interview with the county newspaper. She'd gone into detail about their reasons for the quieter-than-usual event. Word of mouth and a couple of social media posts had spread the news.

Almost all of the veterans Emilio had gotten to know in the past month were here, even those who had said they normally hid out during Fourth of July celebrations. They seemed to be having fun, some with their families and some clustered around a picnic table together, eating and telling stories.

As the event went on, Kitty finally began to look relaxed. She stood in the little gazebo, leaning against the railing, surveying the scene.

Emilio approached her. "Sit down and have something to eat," he suggested.

"I'm too keyed up to eat much, but I do

have my eye on Marla Mangione's apple pie." She scanned the area, turning slowly from side to side. "I can't believe it, but things seem to be going okay."

"Of course they are. You organized everything, and you're good at it." He really wanted to offer her a congratulatory hug, but it didn't seem appropriate.

Yet. Maybe later.

As the sun sank toward the horizon, some of the families with young kids started leaving. Most of the townspeople stayed, content to chat with their neighbors, snag one last hot dog or congratulate the winner of the pie-baking contest while they waited for the dancing to start.

"I'm so glad you thought of having the veterans speak," Kitty said to him. "And that it's happening at sunset. I feel like people aren't ready to go home yet."

"Yes, we need some closure," Emilio said. He was hoping everything came off okay.

Kitty got everyone's attention, speaking into the microphone in a low, clear voice.

Her middle school teaching experience seemed to be serving her well. She introduced the two veterans they'd talked into speaking—one a grizzled Vietnam vet, the other a young woman who had lost part of her leg in an IED explosion and now used a cane. Both of them thanked the community for holding a celebration that they could enjoy rather than avoid.

The townspeople clapped loudly, most standing. Some had brought sparklers and waved them around. The female vet had a great voice, and her a cappella rendition of "God Bless America" had many in tears.

After the short presentation, vendors started gathering their wares and shutting down their booths. Most of the crowd stuck around to help with cleanup or continue socializing.

Suddenly, someone yelled, "No fireworks? This stinks."

The crowd's noise died down as people turned to look toward the side of the gathering. A tall, broad-shouldered man wearing camo was headed toward the stage. There was something off about him.

Emilio glanced at Jake, who looked as concerned as Emilio felt. They both jogged toward the man. Emilio would never have thought anything violent could happen in River Haven, but these days, safe was better than sorry.

He saw a few other people glancing at one another, and a couple of the younger vets joined him and Jake, striding toward the man as he got closer to the stage.

Suddenly, Emilio realized that Mason was running toward the camo-clad guy, too. Emilio reached out to stop him, but he evaded Emilio's grasp. He reached the man and tugged at his arm.

In a panic, Emilio ran toward the pair.

No one else did. When he heard Mason's words—"Dad, no!"—he understood why.

This man was Mason's father, Kitty's ex. He seemed to be out to ruin tonight's event the way he'd ruined last year's. The man pulled his arm out of Mason's grip and continued toward the stage. To

Emilio's relief, he didn't seem to be carrying a weapon.

When Emilio reached Mason, he looked around for Kitty. This was her show and her choice of how to manage it. He'd stay close and make sure they were all safe.

She came to the edge of the crowd, her forehead creased, tension in every line of her body. "Mason, back here."

Mason ran to her, and she hugged him to her side and spoke softly to him.

Meanwhile, her ex was climbing the steps to the stage, waving his arms, raving about the lack of fireworks, apparently trying to ignite people into a protest of the event.

Emilio had to do something, and fast.

Kitty stood beside Mason in the front row of the people clustered around the stage. She wanted to move, to grab Jeff and stop him, but she felt frozen in place.

Her emotions churned. Everything she'd worked for was about to be destroyed.

Jeff reached center stage, stumbling a

little. He started yelling slurred insults about the type of town this was and the lack of patriotism indicated by the tame celebration.

What on earth had possessed him? She knew he'd felt angry about the locals' reaction to him, had felt like he'd been run out of town after his awful performance at last year's Fourth of July event. And he was definitely one to hold a grudge. Still, she'd never expected he would take his hostility to this extreme. Never expected him to do something that would obviously hurt his son.

He was wearing his old fatigues, and she was mortified, especially in front of veterans who served honorably. Especially in front of Emilio, a real hero. It was more stolen valor. Jeff should never have worn anything remotely military again.

Around her, townspeople were murmuring. Were they on Jeff's side? Her ears were ringing too loudly for her to track their words.

Of course they were going to chime in.

They hadn't really been behind a celebration without fireworks, despite their kind words during the past week. She put an arm around Mason. "Be strong. We know we're patriotic, even if nobody else does."

Mason was looking around, leaning forward to listen. Slowly, his tense shoulders relaxed. "They're on our side, Mom," he said.

"Who's on our side?" She was watching Jeff as he raved on. How had she ever found this man appealing enough to marry? She felt like a different woman now.

"Everyone!" Mason said. "Our friends. They're on our side."

"They *are*?"

"Listen!"

So Kitty tuned in, focused on the crowd around them and realized that it was true. The shouts weren't directed against her and Mason, but against Jeff.

"Get off the stage!"

"We'll celebrate how we want to!"

"You ain't no hero!"

A couple of people near her came over and put a hand on her shoulder or shook their heads and patted her back in sympathy.

Emilio and her brother looked at each other, then nodded and climbed the steps to the stage. Jeff was lifting his hands, palms up. "You people are boring!" he shouted.

Emilio and Jake glanced at each other. They spoke to Jeff. Then they each took one of Jeff's arms and escorted him off the stage.

He barely struggled, seeming to know he was beaten.

Thunderous applause broke out.

Someone started singing "My Country, 'tis of Thee." Guitars joined in, and after a moment Kitty realized that all the musicians, amateur and pro, were playing along.

She took deep breaths and tried to understand it. People in town were actually supportive of the celebration that they'd planned. They weren't on Jeff's side, but on hers.

Nora came and stood beside Mason. "Wow," she said. "I always thought I wanted to know my dad, but I can see it's not always so great, huh, kid?"

"For real." Mason looked up at Kitty. "Do I still have to have my visit with him, Mom?"

"Definitely not. He can visit you at the guesthouse or in the yard. Only if you want him to." Jeff would be sleeping it off tomorrow, but she would have some choice words to say before letting Mason even go to lunch with him.

Beside Nora, Alice patted Mason's leg and smiled up at him. "It okay, Mason."

"Can you watch her?" Nora asked Mason. "I have something to do."

"Sure," Mason said. He sat on the ground, and Alice plopped down next to him.

Nora disappeared and then reappeared, talking to Kitty's father.

It seemed like everyone was coming together on this Fourth of July.

An older Vietnam vet took the stage. "Some of us wanted to express our appreciation to this community for taking our needs into account," he said.

People started cheering and yelling their support of the veterans.

"We want to thank Kitty MacIntyre and her crew for planning this great celebration. Kitty, come on up here."

Reluctantly, she walked up to the side of the stage and waved out at the crowd. The cheers and applause were thunderous, and Kitty could only look around and blink against the tears that were coming to her eyes. She couldn't believe it, but the community was on her side and really had enjoyed the celebration.

"We also want to thank the Robinson family," the veteran went on after the applause finally died down.

Hank, the twins' dad, waved from where he was standing in the midst of the crowd.

Nora, though, took his hand and started tugging, forcing him to the stage.

Kitty looked around for Emilio. Did he see this? Was he upset that Nora was communing with the Robinson family?

"This man's our biggest donor," the veteran on stage went on.

Donor for what? Kitty wondered.

"We all chipped in, though."

Chipped in on what?

"Look," someone said in an awed voice. There were gasps, and people pointed to the sky.

Patriotic music started up again.

Kitty followed their gaze and was stunned to see a formation of drones in the shape of an American flag.

Chapter Seventeen

As the drone formation morphed into a flag that was actually waving, Emilio let out the breath he hadn't known he was holding. What a night.

He hadn't been sure the small drone company they'd hired at the last minute would be able to pull it off, but from the oohs and aahs of the crowd, it was working.

In the distance, Kitty's ex was being walked away by a couple of cops. Knowing River Haven, he wouldn't be arrested, just warned against public drunkenness and told to lie low—and not to drive—until he sobered up.

"Uncle Emilio! Come sit with us." It was Nora, beckoning to him. He hustled over to where she, Mason, Alice and Kitty were sitting on a picnic table, staring up into the sky.

The drones rearranged themselves into a simulation of fireworks.

The best part was seeing the amazement and delight on Kitty's face. This whole event had been stressful for her, and her ex showing up had just made everything worse at the last minute. Hopefully that situation had been taken care of and she could just enjoy the show.

When he got closer, he could tell she *was* enjoying it. Was thrilled, in fact. Her hair tumbled down her back, and she held hands with Mason. Alice was in her lap, and she looked so joyous and loving and excited, staring up at the drone-filled sky.

If Emilio could put that expression on her face on a regular basis, he would be a happy man.

Oohs and ahs came again as the drones formed into an eagle taking flight.

Next to Kitty's group, six or seven of the older vets had gathered, including a couple who Emilio knew had avoided celebrations like this in the past because of the trauma. Now they could be included, and they were having a great time. The fireworks issue had brought them together, and they'd put their hearts into raising money for the drone show. Tonight they were as amazed as the rest of the crowd to see what the drones could do.

He nudged Kitty and nodded over at the vets. When she saw their delight, her face lit up even more. "They're loving this," she said. She looked at him, a flicker of concern crossing her face. "It doesn't bother you?"

"Nope. No noise, no explosions. It's all good."

"I don't know how you did it, but it's amazing." She smiled at him, her face friendly enough that he sat down next to her to enjoy the show.

After it was over, friends and neighbors

surrounded them, congratulating them on the show.

"That was cool," one of Mason's friends said, high-fiving him.

"Best Fourth of July ever," a couple of people said.

"Even before the drone show, it was great," said Mrs. Stiffler, the town gossip.

Mrs. Michaelson, who'd been critical of the decision against fireworks, nodded her agreement. "Such a sense of community," she said.

Even the veteran dad of the kid who'd teased Mason gave her a thumbs up.

Gemma came over and hugged Kitty. "Sorry your ex showed up," she said. "Glad you got rid of him." She offered a fist bump to Emilio.

People were thumping him on the back and congratulating him for his role in the show. He noticed that Hank Robinson was also surrounded by happy people, thanking him, and the vets were mingling in the crowd, getting their share of thanks as well.

After the chaos died down and the co-ordinator of the drone show had assured him they had the cleanup under control, he took Kitty's hand. "Can we chat for a minute?"

She looked around. "The kids?"

He pointed to where Nora, Mason and Alice were headed toward home. Mr. Wright was walking with them, along with Jake and Summer and their kids. "They all agreed to take charge for a little while," he said. "I wanted to talk to you. Maybe over here?" He gestured toward a bench that was sheltered in a little archway of flowers and ivy. Moonlight shone through. The crowd was thinning out, and nobody was nearby.

Privacy. Good.

"I don't know where to start thanking you," Kitty said. "I'm assuming you were in charge of the drone show, but how did you pull it off?"

"I had a lot of help. The vets took up a big collection down at the Legion, and there were other donors in town. Hank

Robinson was the big-ticket donor, though, and it was Nora who talked him into it."

Kitty's eyes widened. "You let Nora go over there?"

He smiled. "Oh, you better believe I was there supervising every minute," he said. "But Nora did the talking, and she was very convincing. She's got quite the ability to make a case."

"I could imagine a law career in her future," Kitty said, laughing. "So he donated enough to fund the show, huh? Wow."

"He's a good man." Emilio had hashed out the Nora-and-Ishmael situation with him, and they'd agreed on a policy of grace, plus very close supervision.

"But I still don't understand. How did you find somebody to do a drone show so late?"

"That was a matter of connections," he said. "Just like when we were looking for a fireworks company. Somebody's brother's wife's cousin—but in this case, it was a real nice group of computer guys trying to get started in this field. They were thrilled for the business. We promised a lot of good reviews if the show came together right."

"Of course! They did great!" She looked at him. "But Emilio…why?"

"That's part of what I wanted to talk to you about," he said. He took her hand. "I wanted to show you that I cared about you by helping. I knew how important the show was to you, and I wanted to make sure it worked out well."

"It was wonderful. I don't know how to thank you."

He waved a hand. "No need to thank me." He studied her face. "How are you doing, given that your ex showed up?"

She clapped a hand over her mouth. "I almost forgot about Jeff in the midst of the drone show," she said. "I saw him being led off by the police officers so…things turned out okay, I guess. I feel bad for Mason."

"Me, too," Emilio said. "Tough to have a dad who makes a bad impression, but

I don't think anyone blames Mason for that."

"I don't, either. Emilio, people were fine with our celebration, even before the drone show. They gave me a round of applause!"

"I should hope so," he said. "You deserve more than a round of applause."

"I'm still surprised about all of it," she said.

They sat quietly for a moment. The park was mostly emptied out now. Aside from the occasional passing car or burst of conversation, it was quiet. The fragrance of roses drifted their way.

She inhaled appreciatively and then looked up at him, and there was a question in her eyes.

They had never resolved anything about their relationship, but it was time. He sucked in a breath of warm, fragrant night air. "I really wanted to apologize to you, Kitty," he said. "That's why I wanted to do something big for you. I never should have blamed you for what happened with Nora. I totally overreacted."

"You did," she said, giving him a mock-severe look. "But I forgive you. You're still just learning to be a guardian to those girls, and it's not easy. And it's not necessary to do a big apology, although I sure do appreciate the drone show."

He ran a thumb over the back of her hand. "That's not all," he said. "There's more I have to say to you."

Kitty's heart pounded like a rock-and-roll drumbeat. There was more? What did Emilio want to talk about?

He took her hand. "I've made a lot of mistakes this summer," he said. "But maybe my biggest one was to give up our friendship. I never want to let that go, and I never will again."

Relief washed over Kitty, followed by a feeling of slight discontent. Was this the "let's just be friends" talk?

She squeezed his hand and looked at his

handsome face. She thought of all he'd gone through, setting up the drone show. Even if he did just want to be friends, she was amazed and grateful. "You're a wonderful friend," she said.

He smiled, but it was a crooked smile. As the breeze kicked up around them, she shivered, and he moved closer to put an arm around her, sharing his warmth. "There's something else on my mind," he said. "The truth is, I want to be more than friends."

She sucked in a breath. Her heart stuttered.

He squeezed her shoulders and then moved away a little so he could look at her. "Hear me out," he said. "I always knew you were great, a wonderful person, but in these last few weeks, I've realized so much more about you. You're beautiful and fun, and you're a terrific companion. You're so good with the kids." He paused, then added, "You're way smarter than me, but then, we always knew you were."

She held up a hand, laughing. "I question that," she said.

"I'm sure of it. And more than that, every time I look at you, my heart just melts. Kitty, I've fallen in love with you."

Warmth suffused her face, and an electrical feeling ran up and down her spine. He'd fallen in love with her? Really?

It felt like a dream come true, but there was still worry, too. "Won't romance ruin our friendship?"

"I've worried about that some, but I don't think so. Is it possible that falling in love could just deepen our friendship? What's better than to marry your best friend?"

Kitty gasped and stared at him, feeling her eyes go wide.

Emilio winced, then smiled another crooked smile. "I didn't mean to say that, not yet."

Inside, Kitty was screaming. *Not yet? Not yet?*

He wanted to *marry* her?

He held up a hand. "Look, as you know

better than anyone, I have a lot of baggage. Most of all, Nora and Alice. They're wonderful girls, but they're not necessarily going to be easy. They have some issues because of what their mom did."

She reached out for his hand this time and squeezed it. "I love your kids," she said. "And it's not like I don't have any baggage. I have Mason, who in my eyes is a complete gem, but he's coming up fast on the teen years. And as you saw tonight, I have a problematic ex."

He nodded slowly. "I guess this summer has made us good at baggage."

"It has." She studied him—the slight wrinkles at the corner of his eyes, that strong jaw, the powerful muscles that he always used to protect and never to hurt.

Emilio was everything she'd ever wanted. And he wanted to marry her?

He tilted his head to one side. "So…do you feel for me that way at all?"

"Oh, Emilio." She leaned in and hugged him, then backed up to look at him. "I feel…so, so much for you. You're strong, you're vulnerable and you're willing to learn. Believe me, that's not very common in men. You take charge when you need to, and you're protective of me and Mason. So… I guess what I'm saying is, I love you, too."

They stared at each other as this new reality formed into an almost tangible cloud around them. He tugged her close and kissed her.

When they pulled apart, he kept her face in his hands. "So…like I said, I didn't mean to do this yet, but I'm absolutely sure I want to marry you. Do you think that could ever happen?"

Kitty felt too thrilled and scared and overwhelmed to answer that question yet, so she asked one of her own. "Will the kids be okay with it?"

"Nora will." Emilio smiled. "She helped me plan this all out."

"Plan what out?" Kitty asked, shocked.

"Plan the drone show as a way to apologize, but she did tell me that you might be in a mood to hear more than an apology afterward."

"She's a smart girl. If she's in favor… well, as Nora goes, so goes Alice. And Mason now, too, a lot."

Emilio nodded. "They seem to do great together, those three. But blended families aren't easy."

"I know." Kitty had seen that from her students' families.

"But," he said, "we've both learned we can do hard things."

She loved that about him, his upbeat willingness to take on a challenge.

There was one more thing. "I'm pretty sure I want to stay here in River Haven," she said. "Mason's settled here, and my dad and brother are here. And, well, I love it here."

"River Haven feels like home to me," Emilio said. "Even more with you in it. I'd love nothing more than to raise a family and build a life together, right here."

He reached for her hand and kissed it,

and then they merged into a hug and kiss that held all the promise in the world.

When she pulled back, she looked at him and smiled. "By the way," she said, "the answer is yes."

Epilogue

Three months later, Kitty and her two best friends were in the bride room at the church. Kitty was straightening her veil while Gemma and Summer buttoned her simple white dress.

Sunlight filtered in through the open window, and the breeze brought a slight fragrance of autumn leaves. Kitty inhaled deeply and closed her eyes. Her wedding day. She could hardly believe it, was so thankful for the blessing of Emilio. And she was absolutely ready for what was to come.

Her dad was going to walk her down the

aisle. He had also taken charge of Nora, Alice and Mason for the moment, giving Kitty a little girl time with her friends.

There was a knock on the door. "Everyone decent?" came a deep male voice.

"Come on in," Gemma called.

Pastor Kevin stepped in and looked over the three of them with an approving smile. "I've never seen three more beautiful women," he said. "Beautiful inside and out. Do you want a prayer before the wedding?"

"Yes, please," Kitty said. She had felt her faith deepening during the past three months of building her relationship with Emilio as well as Nora and Alice.

So Pastor Kevin prayed for their marriage, for love and families, and for all of them—Summer, happily married, and Gemma, determined to stay single.

After he left, Summer frowned. "Pastor Kevin seems a little sad. Do you think he'll ever get married again?"

"He should," Gemma said. "He's great.

I'm sure there are plenty of women in the church that are interested. But so far, he seems to dodge them."

Kitty studied Gemma. There was a little crease between her brows, a little sadness in her eyes. "Your turn is next," she said to her friend.

Gemma shook her head emphatically. "You two are a good advertisement for marriage, but no way. Been there, done that. Not doing it again."

Kitty glanced at Summer, and unspoken communication passed between them. They were going to be there for their friend, single or married. And they would help her find love if she wanted it.

Gemma narrowed her eyes and frowned at the two of them, then changed the subject. "Kitty. You're sure you're not sad about not having a real honeymoon now?"

"Nope. I'm super excited about what we're planning, trips and the future generally. Not a sad bone in my body."

Kitty and Emilio were going away just for the weekend, to a luxury lodge in

Cook Forest. They would do a longer honeymoon later, when their jobs allowed it and the kids were secure. Kitty was back teaching. Emilio had a new job at the VA, and was taking counseling classes part-time.

Meanwhile, they planned to take some weekend trips as a family, to make up for the fact that the girls had never done any traveling. All the historical sites in Philadelphia, since Nora was studying American history this year. Amish country, so Alice could ride in a buggy like the ones in her favorite picture book. And Hershey Park, since it was Mason's favorite place, and he was eager to show it off to his new sisters.

Summer peeked out the door, then beckoned for them all to come see. Kitty looked out, and her heart melted.

Emilio was kneeling between Nora and Alice, an arm around each girl, talking to them seriously. Alice said something that made all of them laugh. Then they shared a big hug.

As she watched him with his nieces, Kitty knew for sure that she had made a good choice this time.

She'd known Emilio practically her whole life. She remembered him as a child. She trusted him implicitly. And now, they'd grow old together. Maybe have another child, if God willed it. Because Nora and Mason were tight, but Alice needed a sibling closer to her own age.

There was time for that, though. Time for them to settle into their lives in River Haven. Time for Nora to find her way in her new school, and for Alice to grow from a toddler to a preschooler and beyond. Time for Mason to share his life with siblings and to learn from a new male role model in Emilio.

Time for better or worse, richness or poverty, sickness or health. And a commitment to make it last as long as they both lived.

Full of love and plans and happiness,

she lifted her eyes heavenward and whispered her own personal, heartfelt prayer of thanks.

* * * * *

If you enjoyed this story, pick up the first book in New York Times *bestselling author Lee Tobin McClain's Holiday Haven miniseries:*

A Home for Mother's Day

Available now from Love Inspired!

Dear Reader,

Thank you for making another visit to the Holiday Haven Guesthouse! As soon as Kitty showed up in the first book in the series, *A Home for Mother's Day*, I knew she needed to have her own love story. And since she and her son, Mason, had struggled through a difficult divorce, I wanted her to have a hero she could readily trust. Enter Emilio, Kitty's old best buddy. It was so much fun watching the two of them go from being good friends to being much, much more.

Emilio is my favorite kind of hero: protective and strong, but with a vulnerable side. Like many veterans, Emilio struggles with the feelings evoked by loud noises and flashing lights, which remind him of his time in war zones. He doesn't like Fourth of July celebrations for that reason, but to get help raising his nieces, he agrees to work with Kitty on the Independence Day event.

Kitty doubts the validity of her romantic feelings for Emilio due to her own difficult history. As for Emilio, his family of origin left him avoiding romance, for fear it will ruin everything, as was the case for his mother and sister. But when two good people come together, love can win out, and that's what happened for these two.

Stay tuned for Gemma's love story, coming at Christmastime. What better place to spend the holidays than Holiday Haven?

Wishing you a happy Fourth of July, however you spend it,
Lee